Nominal Cases

Nominal Cases

Thomas Cotsonas

Black
Lawrence
Press

www.blacklawrence.com

Executive Editor: Diane Goettel
Book and cover design: Amy Freels

Published 2016 by Black Lawrence Press.
Printed in the United States.

Acknowledgment is made to the editors of the following journals in which some of the stories in this book originally appeared in somewhat different forms: "René Renée" in *Web Conjunctions*; "Borges' Pseudonymous *Yellow Book*" and "The City's Father" in *751 magazine*; "א; Or the Story of Isaac and His Mother" in *Construction*; "Colloquy" in *Down & Out*; "Avow," "Deposition," and "Zeno's Parachute" in *Western Humanities Review* (as "Three Microstories"). "Little Private Systems" appeared in somewhat different form in *Ochreville* (State University of New York College at Brockport, 2006) as part of my Master of Arts dissertation.

For John Francis Loughney
&
for Karina

Contents

Company	3
Questionette	6
René Renée	13
Mapmaking	22
Avow	35
Borges' Pseudonymous *Yellow Book*	39
Quartet (1)	45
The City's Father	53
RM: A Slideshow	58
א0; Or the Story of Isaac and His Mother	89
Quartet (2)	96
Walts Waltz	100
Colloquy	
I. Anecdote of the Bar.	112
II. Bend Over Backward.	113
III. Mimesis.	117
Little Private Systems	120
Field Notes	132
Walt's Waltz	143
Quartet (3)	148
Deposition	156
Quartet (4)	161
Zeno's Parachute	167

I, the solemn investigator of useless things…
—Fernando Pessoa (as Álvaro de Campos), poem #445

Everything happens by means of short cuts, hypothetically…
—Stéphane Mallarmé, Preface to "Un Coup de Dés"

…[I]t is difficult to discover any objection to a forged Vermeer, except that Vermeer did not paint it…
—Hugh Kenner, *The Counterfeiters*

My father has a red bandana tied around his face covering the nose and mouth. He extends his right hand in which there is a water pistol. "Stick 'em up!" he says.
—Donald Barthelme, "Views of My Father Weeping"

COMPANY

Harold Cornelius Eccles was watering the yard from the patio, standing thoughtlessly there, unconsciously moving his pale denuded arm
back and forth so as to spread the hose's stream over patio plants
and shrubs, the rose bushes and the vegetable garden, the marigolds
and pansies, and back again to the yard itself just in front of him as
he stood there, outside himself but not, forty-one, Vice Executive
Accountant to the Executive Accountant of the company's coming
merger with Ace Pharmaceutical, in a crisp white short-sleeve but-
ton-down shirt and khakis, looking hale but not willful, kind but not
pathetic, a numbers man, a brown-paper-bag-for-lunch kind of man,
a breakroom man who reads the *Wall Street Journal*'s Sports section
first, ten years married/seven years a father, standing there, his back
to his wife Ellie and young son Ivan, both of whom sit cross-legged
and patient on the floor playing Boggle in the cool of their air-conditioned stone colonial on Briar Hill Road in Gladwyne, Pennsylvania
on Philadelphia's Main Line, a Neighborhood Watch Community,
Volvos and Audis and Saabs, tax-deductible hybrids and winding
roads in the watershed of the Schuylkill, a neighborhood of longtime
neighbors and old money and private schools with names like Haver-
ford and Bryn Mawr, around which exists much potential influx,

many potential shareholders, all of whom have sculpted yards and meticulous houses and pretty-but-not-stunning wives with hale but willful children who are often left to their own devices on days like this, hot August days that are good for watering the yard or letting the sprinkler water the yard or calling up the gardener maybe even though it's Sunday to water the yard, in which case it might not be a bad idea to have a drink, some Scotch or a microbrew, because that's what men do is it not, that's what these men do, these briefcase-carriers and R5-riders, inhabitants of this little valley upon which the August sun shines erumpent and hostile and cloudless, in this the Two Thousand and Ninth Year of Our Lord, Anno Domini, a year before the merger, a year before Harold's promotion to Executive Accountant, a year before his move upstairs to Corporate, a year before Ivan's inconceivable, out-of-nowhere, thumbing-the-nose-at-the-father-type mastery of Byzantine economic theory even he, Harold, a Vice Executive Accountant, had found difficult and convoluted and reflexive, before other things, before Ellie quit teaching and took up raising Ivan full-time, before nights turned into weekends and weekends into weeks without Harold seeing Ellie & Ivan at all, Ivan their Gifted Child, Ivan who needed to be scuttled around the country to various competitions and universities, many of which competitions Ivan won, before this, before Harold found himself masturbating regularly for the first time in years, before he started renting an apartment in Rittenhouse Square so he wouldn't need to go all the way back to the empty house in Gladwyne in the evening, before the long exhausting work nights that helped enable this purchase, before Molly, Molly from Corporate, Molly from Corporate whose wrists were small and insect-like but also somehow pretty, before her, before others, before he felt himself cliché, before all this, before everything, before before:

Harold was watering the yard from the patio and felt, for the first time, as if he were himself and something else, himself and someone else perhaps, a thing for which he had no coherent language in any case, a frameless thing among other frameless things, a condition that led him to continue standing there watering the yard for the better part of the day, just beyond the length of Ellie & Ivan's Boggle game in fact, a game that took close to three-and-a-half hours to complete, a game that Ivan won and upon winning ran hurriedly upstairs to record in his journal, an activity Ellie seldom ever had to push him to do, an activity she had done as a child and still sometimes did as an adult and that she often urged Harold to take up but he didn't, couldn't, just as he couldn't do anything now, just as he couldn't move, just as he stood there ankle-deep in a pool of water gathering on the patio, just as later Ellie stood behind him calling his name, Harold, asking him repeatedly just what it was, exactly, he thought that he was doing—a question for which he said that he was certain he had no definitive answer.

QUESTIONETTE

On a scale of 1 to 10—1 being the worst, 10 being the best—how would you say you feel today? At what age, on average, would you say points of embarrassment about one's character become points of pride about one's character? What does it mean to you to be original? Do you take it for granted you're the only life form on earth that's able to think critically about itself? How often do you think about thinking? Did you know Einstein's brain was preserved, studied, and sliced without his family's knowledge or consent? Can babies be cruel? Do you think math and/or music is god's language? Have you ever been to an outdoor sporting event? What about an outdoor concert? Do you give money to charity? Have you ever seriously wondered what it's like to be homeless? How do you shave: with the grain or against it? Do you shave? If given the option of soup or salad right now, which would you prefer? How do you get to work: a) drive; b) bike; c) walk; or d) public transit? Do you work? Do you go by your first name, your middle name, or some other name? Are feelings something you can trust?

How often—if ever—do you write Letters to the Editor of any publication? Do you enjoy videogames? Would you say that you and your siblings—if you have siblings—are friends? When's the last time you spoke to your parents—if your parents are still alive—because you wanted to, not because you felt you had to? Is there any difference between a film and a movie? How many suits do you own? Who really likes hollandaise sauce? Do you believe in astrology? Does it really even matter who killed JFK—shouldn't we be more interested in why he was killed? How often do you brush your teeth: once a day? twice? more? less? Do police interrogators think in questions more often than the rest of us? Do you believe in ghosts?

What about breakfast: is it actually the most important meal of the day? Do you say "dinner" or "supper"? Why do some people say they're standing "in line" while others say they're standing "on line," and further, which is correct? Isn't Freud just kind of full of shit, don't you think? How many hours of television would you say you watch in an average week? Is it okay there's such a thing as agri-business? Why do we call all tissues "Kleenex" and all cotton swabs "Q-Tips"? Are you one of those people who say they don't see race? Is it really necessary to have so many highways? What percentage of people would you say leave the bathroom without washing their hands? Has god ever spoken to you? If so, what did she/he/it say, and in what language?

If you own a car, how often do you use the parking brake? What's the measure of a good day? Have you ever wondered what it might mean to actually lose time? If someone tells you to "get your head straight," what exactly do you think they mean? If you knew Mark Zuckerberg somehow, do you think you'd call him an asshole to his face? Have you ever wondered how it feels to be waterboarded? Would you leave the country if they reinstated the draft? How many of us, when we get right down to it, would take our own lives if we had concrete knowledge of some kind of afterlife in which suicide wasn't punishable? Do you talk on the phone and/or text when you drive? At what point does perception become memory? Is a dog's memory purely sensory? Have you ever been assaulted? Do you think you've maybe done something wrong somehow when, after wiping your ass, there's nothing on the toilet paper, or do you think it was just a perfect dump? Are multivitamins helpful?

Isn't it really just kind of silly that movie stars and athletes make so much money? How is it even possible we haven't blown each other up at this point? Are you an optimist? Do you believe in global warming? How many languages do you speak? Did you know Victor Hugo wrote in the nude and had his butler hide his clothes so he'd be forced to stay inside and do his work for the day? What's the point of procrastination? Can you quantify boredom? What if we had no memory at all—how would language work? What kind of person becomes a policeman? If we know we can never know the answers to certain questions, why do we continue to ask those questions? Is it possible to measure confidence? Why does pain exist? And disease: what's its point? Is it possible to cry yourself to death? What about laughter: can we laugh ourselves to death or would we just die of something like dehydration or malnutrition first? In either of those cases, would laughter be listed as an accomplice? Did Joyce really think people were going to read *Finnegans Wake*? Why haven't more people jumped into the Grand Canyon in an attempt to kill themselves? Can you say, in 100 words or fewer, what the phrase "life-changing experience" means to you? Are you an organ donor?

Isn't it obvious at this point that the person Jesus Christ probably wouldn't have been white? What does it mean when people say we should leave the market alone because it will eventually correct itself? How do you explain the sensation known as déjà vu? Are there degrees of truth or are things just simply true or simply false? If someone tells you you're a cliché and that bothers you, how do you go about trying to fix it? If you're standing on a street corner waiting to cross and a stranger walks up and punches you in the face, do you punch them back? What's the point of art? If there are, say, two paintings in a room, and one of them is a real painting by a famous artist and the other is the same painting by an amateur, and then several well-respected critics come in and agree that one of them is the real painting and the other is a fake, does it matter if they're wrong? Isn't it clear at this point that anybody seeking public office is unfit for it? If you steal something from a store at the age of, say, eight but then pay for it several years later at the age of, say, thirty-two, is it still considered stealing? Why can't Texas be its own country? What about Québec? If people always get better after taking a placebo, can that thing still accurately be called a placebo? Have you ever prayed—genuinely? When we say "I wish I was someone else" does it occur to us we're speaking nonsense? Do you think linearly or associatively? What's the difference? Do the galaxies rotate? If so, in what direction? Does "direction" even make any sense in this context? Which one: right brain or left brain? Is it impolite to clip your nails in public?

If someone says, "Who are you?" what's the first thing you think of to say in response? Do you say your name? Do you tell them what kind of work you do? Do you tell them where you're from or where you live? How do you explain yourself? What if you were not you? What if, say, you were still you, but then somehow, one day, when you woke up you were not you, you were someone else? Which is to say: what if you were you, but also some kind of entity called "not-you"? What if, for example, you had always felt you were a man, but then one day—or over time, it doesn't really matter—one day you realized you were not a man at all you were a woman instead? Or no, what if, for example, you'd been living your life as a priest—or a pastor, or a bishop, or a rabbi, or a nun, any of these are fine, really…a person of god, how about that?—what if, for example, you'd been living your life as a person of god, but then one day you realized you were actually not a person of god at all, you were an atheist instead? What would you do? Would you change your life and become an atheist or would you hold onto your faith and continue to be a person of god? Or no, how about this: what if you'd been living for, say, thirty-three years as a US citizen, but then one day you received a call from a French private investigator who explained to you in French-inflected English that when you were born the hospital staff mislabeled you and got you mixed-up with another baby, and that this mix-up happened to be an international one because the baby you were confused with was actually the son of a French couple who'd been living in the US for several years at the time of his—and your—birth, so that now, talking on the phone with the French private investigator, you realize you grew up with the wrong parents in the wrong house in the wrong city in the wrong country, and that you are not an American at all, really, you're a Frenchman, and your co-mixup-ee, he of course also grew up in the wrong life, which means he's actually not a Frenchman at all, really, he's an American—what about that, for example? And what if it made sense to you somehow? What if, upon finding out about your true Frenchness, you started to feel more French? What would you do? Would you embrace it or reject it? Would you call your co-mixup-ee on the phone or send him an email or write him a letter asking him if maybe you could talk to him sometime? Would you try to meet up with your real parents? What if, at first, your feeling more French only made sense in the form of, say, taste in food, or taste in music or art, some of which tastes were already pretty French-seeming anyway, but that later, after having been aware of your true Frenchness for a while, you started to realize it went deeper than all that? Like, for example, what if all of a sudden—and this is all still just hypothetical of course, but still—what if, all of a sudden, when you spoke, your English sounded French-inflected like the French private investigator's? And then what if it got worse? What if you started dreaming in French somehow, and in the dreams the French made sense to you? What about that? And then what if, through some kind of unexplainable DNA-level thing, your English actually started to deteriorate at a rate equal to and in direct inverse relation with your rate of acquisition of French, so that eventually you couldn't speak English at all anymore you could only speak French? What would you do then? Would you move to France and be French, or would you stay in the US and be a Frenchman abroad? And what if you had a family? How would you explain all this to them? Wouldn't they think you were faking it for some strange and unacceptable reason, probably? Would you hire a translator for this explanation session? If you decided to stay, would you keep this translator on board in order to try to make it work? Or would you take English classes to try to become more American again? Perhaps you'd just abandon your family and use this as an opportunity to start over, as a kind of free pass to try and find that thing you'd always felt had been missing from your life, as a way to do whatever it is you've always wanted to do, whatever that thing may be, perhaps? If you did do this, how would you think about your abandonment of your family? Would you consider it somehow fundamentally different from the abandonment of the more conventional deadbeatdad-type abandonment? If you could consider your abandonment somehow fundamentally different from the more conventional deadbeatdad-type abandonment, would you try, then, to be a kind of better person as a Frenchman than you had been as an American? Of what would this consist? If you succeeded in becoming a better person, if you were able to quantify that somehow, if you were able to come up with some criteria that made sense to you as a reasonable criteria for what it means to be a better person, would you then be pleased and satisfied, or would it still feel as if something was missing? What if your answer to this question was a matter of life and death? Do you think you'd be able to come up with a meaningful answer on the spot? Would you be brief or prolix? Would you try to say exactly what you meant to say, or would you just try to get your point across? What, for example, do you think someone like, say, the person Jesus Christ would do? What about Kant; or, say, Dostoevsky? Or even better: what would a Frenchman do? An American? Is there any difference? In answering this matter-of-life-and-death question would you express remorse? Or, differently put, would you be sorry? Are you sorry? Why or why not? To what end? If you are sorry, how does it feel? Does it help? Do you "trust" it, this feeling sorry? Do you "trust" it? Well, do you?

Answer in as many words as necessary.

RENÉ RENÉE

It is not too difficult to imagine that the following actually happened. Whether it did or not I'm still turning over in my head. Either way, the fact of the story's existence is inarguable, if for no other reason than that one day I was sitting at my desk, wondering when a week-long battle with my sinuses would end, when the story I'm about to tell occurred to me. Unlike most stories, it came fully formed; it was less a damaged infant than a healthy, stable child, and being something of an amateur fiction writer, I thought I'd better get it down at once.

The story is about a woman who is dreaming she is dreaming, and who in the dream's dream wakes herself up because she knows she is frightened of dreaming. She doesn't know why she is frightened of dreaming, but she does know what she feels when she wakes from a dream. It's a sickness, an influenza, she thinks; a parasite that doesn't hurt but weakens, makes her legs feel like liquid, her bones like ropy nooses, her head as a balloon. She has dark hair and her given name is Renée Renault. She works as a data processor in a large office building in Manhattan and takes the 2 train from Eastern Parkway near the Botanic Garden in Brooklyn to 34th Street every day, including weekends. She is prone to bouts of insomnia and is certain this has everything to do with her fear of dreaming. She has tried to locate the point in time when she first became aware of the fact of her fear of dreaming, but every time she does this she starts to feel the fear itself, or what she thinks might be the fear, which in turn makes her feel the sickness again, the one she feels upon forcing herself awake when she's realized she's begun to dream. The woman is very smart. She is well aware that there is probably something awful that occurs in her dreams, and that this is why she is frightened of dreaming. The woman can never under any circumstances remember her dreams when she wakes. Sometimes she considers it a remarkable thing that her brain has made it so she doesn't have to continuing dreaming when she dreams. It's as if her brain feels for her, she thinks, has sympathy and empathy for the fear she feels in a way that other human beings simply couldn't if she were to express this fear to them. The woman has a fondness for balloons. She likes balloons of all shapes and sizes and keeps a party-size one floating in the corner of every room of her apartment. When one balloon starts to sink to the floor she blows up another one and puts a string on it and leaves it in the corner to float. She likes red balloons best, but this is not because she has seen the famous short film *Le Ballon rouge* or because she enjoys the '80s pop hit "99 Luftballoons" by the German singer Nena. It is, instead, because when she was a little girl growing up in Flushing, her father took her to the Guggenheim one day. Her father was a painter. He loved, more than anything else, the Guggenheim's collection of paintings by Paul Klee, and he said to her as they rode the train that day that he wanted to show her something he loved, and that that's why they were going to the museum to see Paul Klee. When the woman thinks of that day now, she only remembers one painting. She remembers standing in front of Klee's *Roter Ballon* and wishing she could reach into the painting and grab the little black dot at the end of the string that went up to the red balloon floating in the middle of the painting, and that when she did she would float away with it, through the space in front of the painting and between her and it, and then into and through the canvas itself, on into some other brown-skied, colorfully geometric, Klee-like world—just as she'd seen the characters do in *Mary Poppins*. The woman also has a fondness for apples. She likes apples of all shapes and colors and sizes, and has little apple knickknacks throughout her apartment. She likes green apples best. This is not because she has a particular fondness for eating Granny Smith apples; nor is it because she enjoys the late and posthumous records of the Beatles that continue to be released to this day by Apple Records, whose logo is a small, shiny-green apple. The woman likes green apples best because of a painting she once made in her father's studio when she was just a teenaged girl. The painting depicts a man in a bluish suit with a red tie and a bowler hat standing in front of a brick wall, beyond which lies the sea and a cloudy sky. The man's face is to a large extent obscured by a hovering green apple with five leaves on its stem. The man's eyes can still be seen; they are peeking over the edge of the apple and are also green. The man's left arm appears to bend backward at the elbow, and his hands look as if they're made of reddish clay. When she finished painting the painting that day, her father came over and asked her where she'd seen it before. This confused the girl, because she was certain the only place she'd ever seen the painting before was in her head, just before and during her painting

of it. Her father started to explain to her that what she'd painted was
a replica of a painting that already existed. He said that this painting
on the easel in front of her looked to be an exact copy of René Magritte's famous 1964 work, *The Son of Man—Le Fils de l'homme*, he
called it. This was unbelievable to the girl, and she insisted that what
he saw on the easel was something she'd thought of entirely on her
own. Her father, being her father and the adult in the situation,
insisted that what she'd really done more than anything else was
demonstrate concretely a remarkable visual memory, an incredibly
detailed and precise visual memory, and that she simply must have,
at some point, seen Magritte's painting somewhere. To this day, the
woman claims she'd never seen the painting before, and she held a
silent grudge against her father for the rest of his life. Her painting
hangs in her apartment above the couch in her living room, and
when guests come over they comment on the Magritte and wonder
how much she paid for it. The woman never tells her guests she
painted it of course, because she knows it would be too complicated
to talk about and that no one would believe her if she told them
anyway. Several years later—after the woman's father had passed;
after she'd moved into her apartment on Sterling Street; after she
took the job as a data processor in Manhattan—the woman was
browsing through the Art section in a bookstore. She'd been browsing for the better part of an hour when all of a sudden she began to
feel ill. She felt weak—as if she might collapse right there in the aisle
unless she found somewhere to sit. Her head began to feel as if it
were expanding outward—as if it were inflating—as if what was
inside was trying to get out. The woman saw a chair at the end of
the aisle and made her way over to it and sat. It was only after sitting

that she realized she'd had a book in her hands when she had started to feel sick. She looked down at the cover of the book and saw it was called *The Surrealists*. The woman opened the book and started flipping through its pages. She saw several things by Salvador Dalí and Max Ernst and Man Ray. She saw Giorgio de Chirico's *La Tour rouge* and Yves Tanguy's *Indefinite Divisibility*. The woman had seen all these paintings before and in fact knew them all quite well. The sickness started to pass as she turned the pages of the book and she began to feel well again. But then something strange happened. The woman turned the page and saw, to her surprise, an exact replica of the painting she had painted as a girl in her father's studio—the painting her father had rightly claimed had already been painted by Magritte, his *Son of Man*, *Le Fils de l'homme*. Yet, when the woman looked beneath the painting she saw that it was not Magritte to whom the book attributed the work; it was, instead, to her, Renée Renault, the Belgian surrealist painter of *Le Fils de l'homme*. This frightened the woman very much, because even though she knew she had in fact never seen Magritte's painting when she painted it herself, she also knew she'd never shown her painting *as her painting* to anyone but her father. And further, she was also the only one who'd ever been in possession of her painting of the painting. So how could it be that as she sat there in the chair in the bookstore that there was a book with a picture of the painting that claimed she had, in fact, painted the painting first, and further that she was a Belgian surrealist and not a New York data processor? The woman began to feel the sickness again. Her legs felt weak and her bones began to feel ropy. Her head was swelling like a balloon. Klee's *Roter Ballon* flashed in her head, and so did the red party balloons in the corners of the rooms of her apartment. She saw an image of her father in his studio. He was shirtless and had paint all over his arms, his jeans, and his work boots. He was on the other side of the studio and it looked to her from where she sat that he was wiping the paint from his brush onto a palette. When he turned and faced her though, she saw that it was not a brush he was holding, it was a knife, and that what he'd been doing was sharpening it with a whetstone. Before she could process what was happening the woman realized that, yes, this was her father standing over her holding a knife, and that, yes, he looked very much as if he was going to use that knife to do something monstrous to her. The woman was so scared she wet herself. She started calling out to him to stop but he didn't seem to hear her or care, and then just as he began to move toward her with the knife, the woman woke herself up. It had all been a dream. And now, sitting in a chair at the end of the aisle in a bookstore in Paris, all was back to normal: he was himself again. He was himself looking at a book entitled *The Surrealists* full of things by Salvador Dalí and Max Ernst and Man Ray. On one page there was a picture of Giorgio de Chirico's *La Tour rouge* and on the next a picture of Yves Tanguy's *Indefinite Divisibility*. The man had of course seen all these paintings before and in fact knew them all quite well. The sickness he'd felt earlier as he stood in the aisle began to pass as he turned the pages of the book. But then something odd happened. The man turned another page and saw, to his surprise, an exact replica of the painting he had painted as a boy in his mother's studio—the painting his mother had rightly claimed had already been painted by Renault, her *Le Fils de l'homme*, *The Son of Man*. Nevertheless, when the man looked beneath the painting he saw that it was not Renault to whom the book attributed the work; it was, instead, to him, René Magritte, the New York surrealist painter of *The Son of Man*. This frightened the man very much, because even though he knew for a fact he had never seen Renault's painting when he painted it himself, he also knew he'd never shown his painting *as his painting* to anyone but his mother.

.   .   .

The story goes on like this indefinitely, Magritte dreaming he read he had in fact painted his own painting in a world where it was true that Renault had painted the painting first, and then waking himself up from a terrible dream in which his mother was about to kill him, only to find it had all been a dream, and that now she was herself again, Renée Renault, dreaming she read she had in fact painted her own painting in a world where it was true that Magritte had painted the painting first, and then waking herself up from a terrible dream in which her father was about to kill her, only to find it had all been a dream, and that now he was himself again, René Margritte... *ad infinitum.*

There's not much else the story could do. And even though it is, to me at least, a frightening story—a horror story—it's less frightening than this: Several weeks ago I was myself in a bookstore and was, myself, browsing the aisles. On this particular day I was in the Reference section looking through something called the *Penguin Dictionary of Literary Terms & Literary Theory.* I happened upon the entry for *surrealism*. I read that *surrealism* was a "movement originated in France in the 1920s and was a development of Dadaism." I also read that the "surrealists attempted to express in art and literature the workings of the unconscious mind to synthesize these workings with the conscious mind. The surrealist," the text continued, "allows his work to develop non-logically (rather than illogically) so that the results represent the operations of the unconscious." I scanned the rest of the entry—I'd learned the term several years ago—and looked instead only for the names listed therein. I found André Breton, Louis Aragon, Paul Éluard, Benjamin Péret, and Philipe Soupault. I also found de Chirico and Ernst and Dalí and Picasso. Still further down, I found Antonin Artaud, Eugène Ionesco, Jean Genet, Samuel Beckett, William S. Burroughs, Julien Gracq, Alain Robbe-Grillet, Nathalie Sarraute, Alan Burns, and B. S. Johnson. I was familiar with all the names on the list; I had read or seen at least one thing done by each of the artists. There was one more name though, one I couldn't possibly have expected: Athanasius Eustace Kotsonis—my given name, the name my parents used for me in our house in Flushing where we spoke only Greek. I read on and found that Kotsonis' primary work was a novel called *René Renée*, which as you now know is the title I've given to a piece of failed fiction I tried to write about a woman who is dreaming she is dreaming, and who in the dream's dream wakes herself up because she knows she is frightened of dreaming.

It ought to go without saying I closed the book immediately and left the store as if I'd forgotten something of great importance that needed to be done at once. I didn't stop walking until I reached the 1 2 3 station at 14th Street, whereupon I sat down on a bench and tried to process what had just happened.

I'll admit to being very scared of absolutely everything over the course of the next twenty-four hours. I called in sick to work and spent my time searching online for anything called *René Renée* and anyone whose name even remotely resembled my own. I called friends and asked if anyone had ever heard of the novel or its author (I go by Thomas, and only my family knows my name is Athanasius). I have yet to find anything that corroborates either's existence, and I haven't been able to bring myself to go back to the bookstore. This is becoming something of a problem. Some books I ordered earlier this month have now arrived, and the clerk keeps calling and asking when I'm going to come pick them up. I always tell him I'll be in tomorrow, and one of these days that will be the truth.

The real problem I'm having is I can't decide if when I finally go in I ought to look in the *Penguin Dictionary* again. If I do look in it, I'm hoping the contents have changed. If things remain the same—or if the book isn't in stock anymore—I have no idea what I'll do with myself. A world like that's a world I'd rather not be a part of. Unfortunately though, the world is more or less real; and I—unfortunately—am more or less Kotsonis.

Mapmaking

—Ezra? Are you awake? Because I'm lying here and I'm awake and I was just curious if I was the only one.

—I'm awake.

—You are? Good.

—

—

—

—Do you think Mom and Dad are awake?

—I don't know, I doubt it.

—I can hear the TV. I think I just heard Peter Jennings say something.

—That doesn't mean they're awake. They sit there with the TV on and fall asleep before they actually get up and go to bed. It's like talking furniture. You know this.

—

—

—

—Why, just by the way?

—Why what?

—Why'd you ask if they're still awake?

—I don't know.

—You don't know?

—I mean I don't know. I've just been thinking.

— Right. And what've I told you about that?

—I know, it's just I can't help it. I can't stop thinking about it, and so I just keep lying here thinking about it and I can't go to sleep.

—

—

—I don't know, man. I guess don't think about it?

—Yeah.

—Yeah.

—

—

—You know what I just thought of just now? You remember that time when I found all that money on the floor in the hotel we stayed in in Hershey?

—

—And remember there were two beds, and you and Harold got the one bed and Mom and Dad were in the other one, and I was on the floor in the sleeping bag between the two beds?

—

—You remember? We were all lying there trying to go to sleep for a while and it was quiet and then I started feeling around under the beds because I wasn't tired and I felt something that felt like money and I said, 'I think I found a dollar.' But then nobody said anything back, so I just kept feeling around under the bed until I felt something else that felt like money and I said, 'I think I found *another* dollar.' And then you and Harold jumped up out of bed and turned on the light and started looking for money all over the place but you didn't find any because I'd already found it all under Mom and Dad's bed. You remember that?

—Yeah, what about it?

—Do you remember it?

—Yeah. What about it?

—Well, I think this thing, I think it's just like that, kind of.

—It wasn't *that* much money. It was like ten dollars.

—I guess.

—It was.

—

—

—But then like earlier that day you guys were all pissed at me because I wanted to go to all the battle sites in Gettysburg and you guys wanted to go to Hershey, and Mom and Dad kept doing what I wanted to do all day instead. I think it's just like that.

—It's probably not like that. And what's this *it* by the way? You still haven't said.

—

—

—Maybe it's not. But then that night, too. You guys wanted to go to bed so we could get up early and go to Hershey but I couldn't fall asleep because of that medicine I was on that Mom always had to crush up in my ice cream. And so I just kept talking even after I found the money because it was weird to sleep in a sleeping bag in a hotel on the floor between two beds. And I knew if I kept talking it'd be less weird and at least somebody'd be awake with me.

—

—

—Okay. But again: what's *it*? From before?

—Well, I was just saying I got to thinking it was the same for you guys. *You* weren't going to feel weird either and somebody'd be awake with you as long as I kept talking. Like the TV. Like I was this noise in the background that was maybe kind of annoying, but also like a reminder, too. You know, that you weren't alone or whatever in this weird place.

—And this is what you're doing now?

—What?

—Demonstrating this theory?

—No, I'm.... Well yeah, I guess. I mean, no yeah, that's what I mean.

—I'm not going to actually sit here and sigh but I will go ahead and say it: Sigh.

—I'm sorry. I can't help it.

—It's all right. I'm just tired.

—See I'm not though. I *should* be, but I'm not. I'm lying here trying to go to sleep but all I can think of is that I'm lying here trying to go to sleep. And I'm anxious too because I've been having these dreams that make me wake up thinking I have no ears.

—Van Gogh.

—They're really pretty scary.

—

—Wait what?

—Van Gogh. He cut off his ear. Ear*lobe*, I guess. That's what I thought of immediately when you said the thing about no ears. Sorry. It's nothing. Ignore me. Go right ahead.

—

—

—

—

—What'd he do that for? Van Gogh.

—I don't know. He was messed up I guess. Sad.

—That's sad.

—I know. People say Gauguin had something to do with it maybe, too.

—What'd Gauguin do?

—I don't know. That's just what people say. Let's just leave it at sad. And go on.

—I forgot where I was.

—The dreams with no ears. And not wanting to go to sleep.

—Oh right. So I've been lying here not wanting to go to sleep, and I was sure for a while it was because of the no ears dreams, which it probably kind of is. But then I got to thinking it was maybe also because I just didn't want to be alone, just me and my dreams about no ears. And then that made me think that that's all dreams really are: just me thinking about me in these really weird and scary ways. And *that's* what made me not want to go to sleep.

—You thinking about you?

—Yeah.

—In really weird and scary ways?

—Yeah.

—You'll get no argument from me.

—What?

—No it's just you sounded just like Dad right there. Like when he counseled me after I quit playing sports? Which is strange because as you were saying it I started to think: 'You'll get no argument from me.' Which is exactly what Dad would've said if he heard you saying what you said just then.

That *is* weird.

—He used to say it all the time.

—I don't remember him saying that at all.

—The best was when he and Mr. Fryer were arguing about the tree line and the sycamore in the backyard that blocked their view. And they left all those angry voicemails on each other's machines and then Dad stopped cutting the yard and everything got overgrown until Mr. Fryer couldn't take it anymore and he gave up and came over and was like 'Sorry about all this. As long as you cut the yard and prune the tree line we'll live with the sycamore blocking our view.' And Dad just looked at him and went: 'You'll get no argument from me.'

—That *is* good.

—Dad's good like that sometimes.

—How old was I?

—I don't know, five or something.

—I don't remember anything before Kindergarten.

—Most people don't. *I* don't.

—That's weird, isn't it?

—Yeah, I guess it is.

—Yeah.

—

—

—Anyway, sorry. Back to your problems. Soldier on. Out with it.

—Where was I?

—Dreams. Dreams with no ears and how they're just you thinking about you in quote these really weird and scary ways and how that's what made you not want to go to sleep. End quote.

—Oh right. Well I also started remembering how last year when Harold was home, how he couldn't sleep at all and how Mom had him take that Nyquil PM stuff and how that made him sleep better.

—So you're taking Nyquil PM to help you sleep better? This is what you're telling me?

—No, not tonight.

—Obviously.

—But I did. I took it the past few nights and it really, *really* worked. Except that then I started feeling this like really intense uneasiness. This really weird feeling that either I was missing out on something or that something really horrible was about to happen at any second. Or both.

—This was at night?

—No, this was during the *day. After* I started taking it.

—D'you tell Mom about this?

—Unt-uh.

—Dad?

—No.

—Why not?

—You know why not. They'd just take me to the doctor or something.

—Oh, that's true; they would do that.

—And I don't want to go to the doctor. I think it's something else.

—Something else? Like what? What else?

—And also I didn't really even know what to say about it till just now. Till tonight.

—And now you want my advice? This is where we're at?

—I don't know. I guess.

—

—

—

—

—

—

—Walt?

—Yeah?

—Stay here.

—Where you going?

—Stay here.

—Ezra, wait.

—Just stay here, all right? I'll be right back.

—

—

—

—

—

—

—

—

—

[…]

—Hello?

—Hello, Walt?

—Harold?

—Walt, this is your brother Harold. I'm in the backseat of a yellow taxicab heading north on Philadelphia's main arterial north-south thoroughfare. Broad Street. Somewhere near...hold on...yes: I just passed over Tasker. So Broad and Tasker, South Philadelphia, Pennsylvania, USA. There's an orange line subway just beneath me. The road, that is. Where are you?

—Where am I? I'm home. I mean I'm at Mom and Dad's. In my bedroom.

—In the city?

—No, Upstate.

—Good, good. I just spoke to Ezra. He tells me you're having dreams without any ears. What's all this about?

—He called you?

—He did, in fact. He called me just a second ago. He's not there?

—No he's not here. I mean he's not *here*, but he's downstairs.

—Fine, fine. Now what's all this about the ears? Are you deaf in your dreams? And am I also to understand that you're concerned about being alone or something? Is this correct?

—Yeah. I mean yeah I guess it is, but—

—No time, no time. Wait. Hey hold on, all right? I need to tell him to make a turn. Can you make a turn here? At the next light? Make a left. Yes, a left at Washington. Good. All right. You still there?

—Yeah, but—

—Okay. Now. Here's what you do: are you listening? Walt? Do I still have you?

—You still have me.

—You're here?

—I'm here.

—And where's here again?

—My bedroom. Mom and Dad's.

—Good. All right. Now here's what you do: you go downstairs and you make some very, very strong chamomile tea. Three or four bags. You boil some water and then you let it steep a minute or two and then you put some honey in it, okay? You following?

—Honey?

—Right, honey. Now. Then you bring it back upstairs and you set it down on the nightstand. You let it sit there for exactly six-and-a-half minutes, and as it's sitting there for exactly six-and-a-half minutes, what you do is you watch the steam. You watch the steam and you think of something very specific.

—Like what?

—Like what, I don't know. Anything. Except not anything. Something you like.

—I like maps.

—Fine, then think about maps. Except make sure it's a *particular* map, and not several all jumbled up. Now. After the six-and-a-half minutes are up and you've thought about your particular map you pick up the mug and you drink the tea very, very fast. Don't worry about burning your throat. The honey won't allow it.

—Is that true?

—It's true. Now after you've downed it, you put it back on the nightstand, you turn off the light, and you lie down and go to sleep. And no fucking Nyquil PM, all right?

—All right. But then what?

—What?

—*Then* what?

—There is no then what. That's it.

—That's it?

—That's it.

—Is that going to work? I mean that's going to help with the dreams and everything?

—I don't know. I hope it does.

—What do you mean you don't know?

—Just that: I don't know. I think it'll work. It works for me. Except as I'm watching the steam I think of myself as a miniature person doing laps in a mug full of vodka. It's actually incredibly—

—But I'm not you.

—That's right. That's *exactly* right, Walt. You're not me.

—This is useless.

—Is it?

—

—*Is* it? … Hey?

—What?

—Who are you?

—Come on.

—You heard me. Who are you? And *where* are you, exactly?

—You know who I am.

—I don't know who you are. Who are you?

—I'm not eleven, you know.

—No? You're not eleven?

—No.

—I haven't got all day here, kid. *Who* are you? And *where* are you, exactly?

—Do we have to do this?

—Yes, we absolutely have to do this.

—Fine. I'm Walter Democritus Eccles, Junior, and I'm thirteen and in the seventh grade at School Without Walls.

—And where are you?

—My bedroom. Mom and Dad's.

—Exactly?

—My bedroom. Mom and Dad's. 27 Vick Park A, Rochester, New York, 14607.

—Good. And where's Ezra?

—I don't know, he just came in.

—So he's in bed?

—He's in bed.

—And where are Mom and Dad?

—They're downstairs sleeping on the couch and in the chair.

—And are you all alone?

—No, I'm not.

—Good.

—Hold on.

—Look I have to go here. I'm sitting in front of my building the last couple minutes and the meter's running.

—Where are you?

—Exactly? I'm at 1512 Spruce Street, in the Rittenhouse Square neighborhood of Philadelphia, Pennsylvania, 19102. I have to go. The meter's getting ridiculous.

—Hold on.

—Be good, okay?

—Okay.

—You're good?

—I'm good.

—All right. You're sure?

—I'm sure, but hold on.

—Goodnight, kid.

—Goodnight.

—[Click.]

—Hold on.

Avow

For a couple of years when I was in my thirties, I lived with a woman who was narcoleptic. It wasn't something she'd always had. It just kind of materialized somewhere in the middle of our first year together. Narcolepsy's not unlike many other sleep disorders in that sometimes it takes a while for doctors to figure out what medication works best. Whatever works for one person almost certainly won't work for another, and no matter what ends up being prescribed in the long run, complete control of all the symptoms is more or less impossible. When I think of her now, one thing that comes to mind is the bathroom mirror and how it seemed like every other week there was something new behind it. Methylphenidate. Dextroamphetamine. Modafinil. These are just three of the names I happen to remember. I'm sure there were many more.

The whole thing was really hard at first. This constant alteration of stuff she was putting in her body for the express purpose of altering it. For one thing, her doctor recommended some lifestyle changes before she even started the medication. One big change was his suggestion she quit drinking coffee. If you are now or ever have been a coffee-drinker and tried to quit, you know how difficult this can be. You get these headaches that seem like they won't ever go away, and there's almost nothing you can do for about a week but take ibuprofen and drink lots of water and try not to go to sleep. Imagine going through something like that at the same time you're being told to take all kinds of new, unwelcome medications. None of which anyone is sure will work, and all of which are stimulants that tend to make you irritable and nervous-seeming all the time. "It's like my own little private corner of Hell," she told me once when I asked how she was doing. There was nothing I could say to that.

Despite all of this, we dealt with things pretty well. She didn't have to stop teaching at all, and during the trial medication period the narcolepsy even manifested itself in a number of humorous ways I won't go into here. I hesitate for a couple of reasons. First of all, it's highly personal—even more personal than, say, our sex life. And second of all, the narcolepsy also manifested itself in some pretty terrible ways too—one really terrible way, in fact, that happened only a couple weeks after we thought she'd been stabilized and they'd figured out that Modafinil was the thing for her.

We were living in a rented apartment in a small town Upstate when it happened. Like most small towns up there, you can't get anywhere or do anything without a car—especially in the rural areas where it's trees and woods and the occasional open field and that's just about it. Anyway, she'd been working pretty late that day grading papers and doing prep work for a lecture. This was normal. I remember she called around seven to say she was on her way home and I could start getting something ready for dinner if I wanted. Well, you can probably guess she never made it. Never even came close. A few miles down the road from the school she fell asleep and her car drifted off the highway and ran into a tree at close to forty miles an hour. By the time I got the call and went down to the hospital she was in critical condition and in no shape to see anyone at all. And then, several hours later, they had to amputate both her legs below the knee.

Our life changed pretty drastically after that. She had to take a leave of absence in order to complete the rigorous physical therapy her doctor recommended, and I took a semester leave—I also worked at the school; I was in the Art department and she was in English—so I could stay home and help with everything she was going through. She was still dealing with the narcolepsy at this point too, if you can believe it.

One night a couple months into our new situation, we were in bed watching TV. The news was on, or one of the late shows maybe, it doesn't really matter. We were just in bed and the TV was on. She was watching it more than me. I might've had a book open, or a magazine. Either way, I was doing one thing and she was doing another when she reached over and touched my arm and looked at me and asked me if I still loved her. I looked at her and said of course I did, and how could she even think of asking such a question? She kept her hand on my arm but looked at the TV again and said she'd understand if I didn't. "Didn't what?" I remember saying. "Didn't love me anymore," she said. She said she'd understand.

We didn't say anything else that night. I kissed her and told her it was getting late and we had to get up early to go to therapy so we should probably try and get some rest. She kept looking at the TV for a while after that and then drifted off to sleep without shutting it off. The volume was way down and the room was that weird luminous blue rooms always are when it's night and TVs are left on. I drifted off then too, and fell asleep sort of half sitting up and half lying down.

Another night, a few weeks later—this was pretty close to the end of it all—we were in bed fooling around. She was on her back—which had been her favorite position even before the accident—and I was on top of her when something strange happened. I watched her bring her hands together over her chest the way people do when they're about to pray. She clasped them there for just a second, and then reached up and put them around my neck and pulled my face close to hers. She kissed me, then brought my ear close to her mouth and said something I didn't understand. She finished almost immediately after that, and then I went about my business and finished too.

Once again, we didn't talk about what happened, didn't talk about what she'd said, whatever it was. But now, when I think about her living in that house—and she still does live in that house—I see her face and it's all distorted. There's a kind of grossly hideous twist to it, as if it's been mangled with a surgical instrument, or just permanently altered somehow, like in one of those funhouse mirrors. This bothers me; this bothers me so much I can't even begin to say. It makes me feel like an awful fucking person. Like I've done something wrong somehow. I don't think I did, but I don't know, maybe that's right. Maybe I am an awful person; maybe I have done something wrong. And maybe I deserve to remember her this way. As penance or something. Maybe I do. That's what penance means, right?

Borges' pseudonymous
YELLOW BOOK

By the time he was 60 in 1959, the Argentinean poet, essayist, and short-story writer Jorge Luis Borges was almost completely blind. Despite this (or perhaps because of it) there are no references to blindness in any of his fiction—which is to say: the debilitating hereditary condition that afflicted the man for much of his adult life never made its way into his most important work. In fact, if we want to find anything on blindness in all of Borges, it's the nonfiction we must look to,[1] or the interviews he gave when he came to the US to lecture in the 1960s. Here—in *The Paris Review* interview with Ronald Christ, especially—we find a happy older Borges at the peak of his international success. He's funny and erudite and esoteric, and when asked about his use of color in fiction, he turns the conversation inward upon himself. He opens up and talks about the "gray world" he lives in now, the "silver-screen world" where yellow is "the most vivid of colors," "the last color to stand out," "the only color [he] can see, practically!" What Borges does not speak of in

---

1. It shows up in some of his essays, and is the subject of his lecture "Blindness," which can be found in the compilation *Selected Non-fictions* (Penguin, $22), edited by Eliot Weinberger.

this interview—or anywhere else for that matter—and what we're only finding out about now in Anthony Kerrigan's stellar translation of *El Libro Amarillo* (*The Yellow Book*) is that near the end of his life Borges had been planning a novel-length work of fiction based on his conception of the condition of blindness and how it relates to human perceptions of color.

Let me repeat that: near the end of his life, Borges—a writer whose longest published story is fourteen pages—had been planning a novel-length work of fiction. This is great news, in and of itself. Unfortunately for us, he never finished it. He never even really started it, actually, but he did leave behind close to forty pages of notes in a small notebook that has its own kind of Borgesian tale to tell. In a stirring introduction by fellow-Argentine César Aira,[2] we learn that Borges kept these notes in a yellow notebook with the initials "A. B. C." on the cover. The first date mentioned in the book is 4 December 1950; the last date is 25 July 1985.[3] This means that within a year of his death from liver cancer at the age of 86—Borges died in Geneva, Switzerland in June of '86—he still thought about and made preparations for the novel outlined in the notebook. The official story, as Aira tells it, is that Borges' family and the executors of his estate had assumed "A. B. C." stood for "Adolfo Bioy Casares," a longtime friend and collaborator of Borges,[4] so they never bothered looking in the notebook. Aira discovered the contents on his own in 2008

2. An avant-gardist who's best known in this country for his surreal novels *An Episode in the Life of a Landscape Painter* and *Ghosts*, both available from New Directions for $12.95.
3. The former is about a year after the Spanish-language release of *The Aleph*, which includes such Borges classics as the title story, "The Immortal," and "The Writing of the God."
4. The two wrote several books and screenplays together, and even invented a kind of double-doppelgänger named H. Bustos Domecq.

while working on a book about the history of Argentinean literature commissioned by the Argentine government.

Four years later, at the end of this week, Penguin will release in the US the first hardcover edition of *The Yellow Book* ($35). If you're a Borges fan at all—which is probably the only audience a book like this has—you might as well just go ahead and buy it. It's worth the price and then some. For starters, translator Kerrigan and the people at Penguin have taken a cue from philosophy books and published the Spanish and English texts side-by-side. The cover is a facsimile of the actual cover of the notebook, and after we get the bilingual printed texts there is a facsimile of all the pages of the notebook itself, just in case you're interested in seeing what a nearly-blind Borges' handwriting looks like.

The Yellow Book opens with the heading, "Notes for a Novel?," and the text that follows is a kind of outline for a story in which a "1st-person narrator named Billy Rubin"—who is a Buenos Aires librarian, of course—"thinks he remembers the quote 'There is little more important than my perception of yellow.'" Rubin is certain he's read this quote somewhere, and he spends the rest of the proposed novel trying to track it down. He neglects his job and family, and in the process becomes a kind of amateur expert on color theory and the history of the color yellow. He even starts keeping a notebook that contains a long list of "Todas las cosas amarillas"— "All Things Yellow." The list and his search consume him. It will "come to define him," Borges writes, and when he finally does find the quote's source—the precise details of which hadn't yet been worked out when Borges died—he sees he's actually misremembered it: the quote reads "There is little importance in my perception of yellow." Borges notes that this will be a key moment, and then, a couple lines down—and apparently two years later, according to the dates—Borges picks it up again and writes "Rubin sits in the library in front of the open book. He is dejected and horrified that the thing he has come to consider the key to his existence is actually just something he pursued almost at random." Rubin then leaves the library and starts walking home. He begins to drift away in thought. His life, he thinks—indeed, all humanity—is little more than an accident, and because he's paying little attention to the traffic of the city, he is struck by a yellow taxicab as he's crossing the street and is, henceforth, blind.

This is the end of "Part I," and, I'm sorry to say, all Borges left us. On the next page he had written "Part II" and the date "25 July 1985," but there is nothing else in the notebook, save what looks like a partial list of the list he'd been thinking Rubin might have compiled. The list is Borgesian in its own right. Some of it is rather obvious—"Gilman's 'The Yellow Wall-paper'," an entry on the wavelength of yellow from Goethe's *Theory of Color*, notes from the *OED* on the origins of the English word *yellow*—but others are downright bizarre: "Yellow=Mondays," "The Beatles' 'Yellow Submarine',"[5] "F. G. W. Struve, 1827, classifies stars according to color: *flavae* (yellow)=spectral range F5-K0." There's a note about the mention of a shield in *Beowulf* made from a yew tree as the oldest known description of yellow, and the final twelve entries that round out the list make as fine an example of Borges' wide range of interests as do the lists of books and authors he compiled near the end of his life.[6] See for yourself:

5. Imagine for a second, if you will, this towering figure of literature sitting down in his Buenos Aires home to listen to *Revolver*…
6. Also available in the *Selected Non-fictions*.

- Mayans associate yellow with the direction of south, and the concepts of preciousness and ripeness
- Yellowcake=concentrated uranium oxide, which is obtained through milling of uranium ore; used in preparation of fuel for nuclear reactors and in uranium enrichment (key to the creation of nukes)
- My neckties!
- Yellow ochre, Indian yellow, Naples yellow, Cadmium yellow, Chrome yellow, Gamboge
- The Tour de France's "yellow jersey" (*maillot jaune*);
- Taxis in the USA—yellow because it is the most vivid of colors (easier to see in fog and darkness than scarlet, which had been the original color they thought of using)
- Yellowstone National Park in Wyoming, USA
- Yellow #5
- Swedish film *Jag är nyfiken—en film i gult* (*I Am Curious (Yellow)*), dir. Vilgot Sjöman
- Lemons, lemons, lemons!
- Yellow bile=1 of 4 elemental bodily humors of medieval physiology; regarded as causing anger, choler
- Tibet → Yellow Hats/Gelugpa

The Yellow Book is decidedly not for those new to Borges. But, for those who know and love his work already, this will make a

fine addition to your bookshelf. For good measure, Aira's introduction also provides a lucid and gripping account of the rigorous
"authentication process" the notebook had to go undergo. He gives
us statements from several Borges scholars—many of whom still
believe the book is a fake[7]—and also suggests ways one might go
about reading the wide variety of material between the book's cov-
ers. *The Yellow Book* ends with a full-text translation of the report
of the investigation conducted by the Secretaría de Inteligencia—a
sort of Argentinean CIA. This too is thrilling reading, and it seems
to mark new ground in the History of the Book and, more specifically, book-forgery. One comes away from it all thinking that, fake
or not, Borges probably would have enjoyed all the confusion.

I read the last part of the book on a downtown Q train,[8] and by
the time I reached Canal Street I was certain this was one of the
saddest books I had ever read. In looking over the facsimiled pages
that contained the older Borges' handwriting I began to feel I was
witness to a kind of strange and fitting paradox: the sharpening of a
brilliant mind in terms of the ideas it was producing seemed to vary
inversely with the way in which those ideas appeared on the page.
Which is to say: what I read had brilliance, but everything looked
as if it had been written by a four-year-old.

Perhaps we can't really know for sure whether Borges is the
author of *El Libro Amarillo*. Even in death he has us grasping at the
truth, and after we feel we've got something in our hands we know
is real and we look down to examine what we we're holding, all we
know for sure is that we don't know.

---

7. Recent Borges biographer, Edwin Williamson (*Borges: A Life*, Penguin, $18), makes
the rather bold suggestion Aira wrote the notebook himself, a claim that Aira patently
rejects, saying simply "This is not my style."
8. A train whose identifying color just so happens to be yellow, by the way.

Quartet (1)

It's 1564. The setting is Mondovì, Italy, a small town in the Piedmont region approximately 80 kilometers due south of Turin and 70 kilometers northwest of the Mediterranean. A man with a beard and a prominent brow sits at his work desk completing what seems to him an ingenious tale. The man is stern and pale, and the premise of his tale is as follows: an ensign in the Venetian Republic lusts hopelessly after the wife of his Moorish superior. The ensign's lust goes unrequited, though, and he feels scorned in the worst possible way a lust-seeking young man can feel scorned, and as a result of this he decides to seek vengeance against the wife. What's also important to know is that the ensign's lust and vengeance-seeking are unbeknownst to the Moor. As far as he knows, the ensign is a close and trusted friend—a compatriot. He's so close and so trusted, in fact, that when the ensign approaches the Moor and tells him he has reason to believe the Moor's wife has been less than faithful to him, he (the Moor) believes the ensign without question. It doesn't occur to the Moor that the ensign might be lying. Because why would the ensign lie? He's a close and trusted friend—a compatriot—and close and trusted friends in the Venetian Republic who also happen to be compatriots do not, as a rule, lie. It also doesn't occur to the Moor that perhaps he ought to ask his wife if these accusations are true. The bearded, prominent-browed author of the tale is unclear about this for reasons that are themselves unclear, and so for concision's sake they won't be explored here.

What the bearded, prominent-browed author is clear about, though, is that it is this particular piece of adulterous information that sends the Moor climbing quietly up the walls. A confident, happy Moor at the beginning of the tale is very quickly transformed into a paranoid, spying Moor who spends most of his time standing behind partitions gripping his fists in rage and seething the way perhaps only a cuckolded man can seethe. He imagines his wife in her bed with other men.[9] She is doing things with these other men he wouldn't even dream of asking her to do with him. To say the Moor is tortured and nauseated is an understatement: he is actually and figuratively beside himself—a truly split personality. And so what the bearded, prominent-browed author gives us then is this strange almost-Jungian situation some 300-odd years before Jung himself, wherein the Moor's "No. 2"—an enraged, furious Moor—has bubbled up to the surface and is functioning right there alongside his default "No. 1"—the kind, sensible, rational Moor. His No. 1 is of course vaguely aware of his No. 2's existence, but there's not really anything he can do to stop it from appearing on the scene. Within hours it becomes clear to the Moor's No. 1 that now, with this piece of information about his wife in his head, he's in a position where if he doesn't talk to someone soon about the way he feels, he's going to do something he might regret.

Because, of course, the Moor considers the ensign a close and trusted friend—a compatriot—it is he who the Moor approaches

---

9. It's 1564, remember. It wasn't all that uncommon for men and women to sleep in separate rooms let alone separate beds.

and asks for help. The two meet discreetly and discuss how the Moor is feeling[10] and what he thinks he might have to do in order to deal with this problem the ensign's been a good enough friend to let him know about. The meeting lasts a while, and it consists of a lot of back-and-forth and confusion on the part of the Moor. Eventually—and not without a little prodding—the Moor agrees with the ensign that there's absolutely no way his wife can go on living. She has, after all, dealt him the greatest of all shames, and he (the Moor) and the ensign will simply have to murder her in order to set things right.

Given what's considered violent versus what's considered entertainment in contemporary television, movies, and video games, one would think that a tale written by a bearded, prominent-browed author in 16th-century Italy would be incomparable. In the case of this particular tale, though, one would be incorrect in that assumption, because here, in this tale, the murder of the Moor's wife is depicted in a way that's shockingly detailed and truly violent. It turns out our bearded, prominent-browed author has something of a fetish for blood and gore, and it's in this way his tale seems thoroughgoingly modern and relevant. The murder reads like a scene Melville might've written in the early-draft stages of *Moby-Dick*, with a young and virile Ahab bludgeoning whales for the sport of it, but that ended up getting tossed out on account of narrative inconsistency.[11]

---

10. The ensign is, indeed, functioning as the Moor's psychologist here. A psychologist with a motive, to be sure, but a psychologist nonetheless. (Besides: don't all psychologists have a motive?)

11. Because: how could Ishmael recount to us anything about a young and virile Ahab, let alone whatever adventures Ahab had had sailing around the globe before the occasion of the book's narrative? It's possible Ahab had told him, yes, but the text of *Moby-Dick* does not support this claim, insofar as Ahab doesn't really appear to talk to anyone except himself, and certainly not someone as inconsequential as Ishmael to the finding and killing of the Whale. On the other hand, Ishmael is almost prototypically unreliable and

But back to the tale: the murder scene begins modestly enough.
The Moor and the ensign knock on the Moor's wife's door and she
answers shyly and asks them in. So far, all seems more or less well
to the Moor's wife. She has, on occasion, had the Moor and the
ensign in her room. Nevertheless, it becomes clear to her almost
right away that this occasion is different, because only seconds after
she's asked them in she hears the door slam and the sound of the
lock behind her, and when she turns and looks at her husband she
sees a kind of rage in his eyes. The Moor's wife is, now, understandably frightened. She begins to back away from the Moor the way
we've all seen cowering women back away from dangerous men on
television and in films. Just like those cowering women on television
and in films, there's only so far the Moor's wife can go before she
runs out of room, and when she does eventually run out of room,
what we see is the Moor's wife trapped in the corner with the Moor
standing over her—*gazing down*, one might say—shouting accusations she can't quite understand. The Moor's wife becomes frantic
then, but so does the Moor; and just as she's about to proclaim her
innocence and confusion, the violence begins. The Moor pulls out a
sand-filled sock and starts bludgeoning his wife in the head repeatedly, which bludgeoning the bearded, prominent-browed author
relates blow by blow, strike by strike, until, one paragraph later, the
Moor's wife is no longer the Moor's wife: she's the body of a woman
who's no longer alive. The Moor isn't done with her, though. Almost
immediately after it's clear she's dead, the Moor sets the murder
weapon down and motions to the ensign to come help him move the

---

does, in fact, give several accounts he couldn't possibly know anything about. Perhaps
the analogy breaks down then?...

body.[12] The ensign comes over and they pick her up from the floor
and place her on her bed where, presumably, they're going to leave
her to be found and mourned by all the people of Venice. This presumption—just as the one before it—the one about a 16th-century
tale being somehow necessarily less violent than current TV, films,
or videogames—is also incorrect. The bearded, prominent-browed
author doesn't stop here: his Moor and ensign are still not through
with the lady—not by a long shot. Instead, what they do next is
they decide it'd be a really good idea to smash the dead woman's
skull. They reason that her crime was one of passion and lust, and
that this passion and/or lust was the product of her brain and her
eyes, and so by smashing the dead woman's skull what they're doing
is ensuring that in the after-life she won't be able to look at any
other possible after-life men. This makes a whole lot of sense to
them. And so now the ensign stands guard again at the door as the
Moor again raises the sand-filled sock and brings it down upon
the already-dead head of his wife until her face is no longer a face
but a pile of blood and bones and ropy sinews and meaty-looking
chunks.[13] Again, reading along, one presumes that surely this is
quite enough; surely the Moor and ensign have done what they had
come to do and will now be on their guilty way. They've killed a
woman for a crime she did not commit, and completely obliter-
ated the woman's face and skull and left her dead upon her bed for
all of Venice to find. Yet again, this presumption is incorrect. The

---

12. It's unclear what the ensign's doing as the Moor murders his wife, but one can probably assume he's standing guard and grinning and rubbing his hands together the way
all villains grin and rub their hands together and say things under their breath like,
"Excellent."
13. One begins to wonder here about the bearded, prominent-browed author's personal
experience with something like this. Not to mention his views of women…

bearded, prominent-browed author decides that not only are his Moor and ensign gruesome and ferocious, they're also really, really smart. Because as they're making their way out of the Moor's dead wife's bedroom, the ensign happens to look up at the ceiling above the Moor's dead wife's bed, where he just so happens to see a large and possibly foundation-crumbling crack. It's at this point that the ensign stops and nudges the Moor and points to the crack and says that this is their way out: this is how they can be certain the murder won't be pinned on them. If they rig the ceiling to collapse it will instead look as if it's *that* that's killed her—that and not the vengeful ensign in ironic collaboration with the Moor. This, of course, is precisely what happens. The family mourns their daughter's misfortune, and Venetian life continues. Nobody suspects the Moor or his ensign. The ensign makes out doubly well here too, because not only has his vengeance been met, it's been met in collaboration with the only true impediment to that vengeance. Things are looking pretty good for the ensign at this point.

Over time though, something happens to the Moor: he starts to miss his wife. He wonders if she'd actually cheated on him, and he begins to associate her memory with the sight of the ensign. Having no idea what to do in this situation—and feeling waves of guilt, the likes of which he never even knew was possible—the Moor decides the only thing he can do is make sure he keeps the ensign very, very far away from him at all times. The best thing he can think of to do this is to demote the ensign, to put him out of his direct charge.

Now, readers of course know this is a terrible mistake. The ensign is devious and cunning and able to carry out violent acts of vengeance with a clear conscience and very little motive. Readers can also guess that upon finding out about his demotion it wouldn't be at all beyond the ensign to plot some sort of parallel plan of vengeance for the Moor himself. But obviously the Moor is unaware of this side of the ensign, and he does in fact demote him and this predictably enrages the ensign and causes him to disclose to his new squadron leader the Moor's involvement in the murder of his wife. As a good man and citizen of the Venetian Republic, the squadron leader can't keep this information private. Word soon spreads that it's the Moor who's to blame for the death of his wife, not the faulty ceiling in her bedroom. The Moor is publicly denounced, arrested, and moved from Venice to Cyprus, whereupon he's tortured and enslaved and told time and again he must admit his role in the crime. The Moor refuses to admit this though, and as a result he's moved into solitary confinement where he's again tortured and eventually executed at the behest of his murdered wife's family.

Now what about the ensign? Why doesn't the Moor implicate the ensign for his role in the murder? Well, as with the part about the Moor just accepting the ensign's disclosure about his wife's infidelity, the bearded, prominent-browed author is silent on this issue. Instead, he tells us that the ensign escapes any punishment for his role in the murder, but that later in life he engages in various other types of crimes and dies a terrible death in a prison yard in Venice, and that's how the story ends.

The bearded prominent-browed author is of course correct in thinking he's just finished an ingenious tale. What he can't possibly know though, is the significance this tale will have for future generations. On the contrary: he's actually quite certain nobody anywhere will ever read the tale, because he knows his recent disagreement with his patron has left him in the rather unenviable position of being a writer in 16th-century Italy with absolutely no money whatsoever in his purse. Despairing, he scours the region for any available teaching posts. After an exhausting search, he secures a chair in rhetoric at a university in Pavia where he stays for three years. Soon thereafter, his health declines, and the bearded, prominent-browed author dies, at the age of 69, an uncelebrated novelist, poet, and academic. His forward-thinking work as a proponent of violence in the arts will not be recognized until later, when in the early 1600s an English dramatist picks up a French translation of the tale and decides to re-write it for the stage. The dramatist changes several things—perhaps the most important of which is the ensign character's role, which in the re-written English stage version has nothing to do with the ensign's erotic interest in his Moorish superior's wife, but instead with the ensign's desire to bring about the downfall of the Moor for having passed him over for a promotion to the rank of the Moor's lieutenant. But this is to be expected: the English dramatist knew the story's violence was too detailed and gruesome for English playgoers of the time, so he focuses much of his attention on creating what is perhaps the most striking example of unprovoked and unnecessary evil in all English literature. In fact, it's often still debated today whether the ensign character's villainy is warranted, given that the only possible reason the English dramatist gives us to explain the ensign's actions is bitterness at having been passed over for promotion.

The city's father

I spent the weekend on my Plan for the City. There was a great deal of back and forth. Major issues as well as minor ones frustrated me. Doubts arose and subsided, and then arose again. My Plan remained unfinished. The new week started and the deadline for the Plan passed. I worried about my place in future City governments. The City's inhabitants grew restless. They sent letters to my office. I opened them and read them and considered their concerns:

> "When will you be finished with the new City Plan?"
> "How will the proposed installation of _____
> affect _____?"
> "How much will this cost us in new taxes?"
> "What do you plan to do about _____?"
> "When will the tolls be lifted on the bridges and tunnels?"
> "Why haven't you done anything about _____
> like you promised?"
> "The issue of _____ is still unresolved, and
> you, sir, must be held accountable."

I began to feel there was nothing I could do. My resources were stretched. I suspected my advisors no longer trusted me. This was confirmed when I called a Meeting of the Cabinet and nobody showed but me. I sat at the head of the table and told myself that this was very bad, this was very bad indeed. I got up from the table and went around to all the offices and found them all empty. I stood there in the main hallway and felt Crisis and Panic and 'What do I do now?' I wondered why I had wanted the job in the first place.

I decided to pull an all-nighter: pizza and coffee and caffeinated colas; legal pads and laptops and tablets; piles and piles of each Department's Official City Files; the candle burning at both ends. I thought deeply about the City's Infrastructure. I tried to re-imagine the City Layout and worked to come up with new ways the City could go about its business. The sun went down and the moon came out; the moon disappeared and the sun came up again. I was haggard. I'd worked two days and two nights, but still had no City Plan. My phone rang; I declined to answer it. I heard knocking on the doors of City Hall; I ignored it and pressed on. My phone rang again, and then other phones rang in other offices in other parts of the building. The knocking grew louder. It was, one might say, a cacophony of ringing and knocking.

o o o

At last I had an idea.

I got up from my desk and went down the main hallway to the doors of City Hall. I opened the doors and greeted the knockers. They yelled and made obscene gestures. I did not blame them. I only asked that they calm down, and told them there would be a Press Conference in an hour. They calmed down and said they would

return for the Press Conference in an hour. I went back to my desk
and prepared a speech.

An hour passed.

At 10:00 a.m., the Press arrived *en masse* with all the inhabitants of
the City. They stood on the steps of City Hall and waited for me to
come out. When I came out they were silent. They looked at me and
waited for me to speak to them. I held the podium tightly. I stood
up straight and looked out at the whites of their eyes. Then I looked
at their faces and their clothes and tried to determine the way their
hearts beat. I noticed some of them held pitchforks and some of
them held burning torches.

At 10:05, I announced my resignation as Mayor of the City. At 10:06,
the celebration started. I had more to tell them, but they had already
heard what they wanted to hear. A shout went up, and soon the
inhabitants of the City sang "For He's a Jolly Good Fellow" as if they
truly felt I was a Jolly Good Fellow. There was dancing and drinking and music and laughter on the City Green for the first time in
a long time. Someone rang the City Bell. I celebrated with them
deep into the night and felt, from time to time, City Pride swell up
in my breast. It felt nostalgic more than anything else. Eventually,
everyone fell asleep on the City Green and on the steps of City Hall.
Before I fell asleep I could tell they were happy, and looking forward
to the City's future without me.

o   o   o

When the sun came up at dawn, I awoke with it. I shuffled back into City Hall to pack up my things. The City's inhabitants slept soundly as I did this. The next few hours were a whirlwind:

At 6:00 a.m., I left the City.

At 7:00 a.m., I changed my name.

At 7:30, I walked into a bank in Another City and made a large deposit in my new account.

At 7:45, I had a cigar.

At 7:50, I sat in my new apartment in Another City and drank some cognac.

At 8:00, the people on the City Green began to rise.

At 8:30, they realized I had sold the City out from under them to a large, Nameless Conglomerate of Interested Foreign Investors.

At 9:00, the large, Nameless Conglomerate of Interested Foreign Investors had ensured I would never be found by anyone who had any interest in trying to find me.

At 10:00, everything was over.

You may be wondering why I told this story. I sometimes wonder that myself. If you're not wondering why I told this story, by all means stop reading and move on with your life and think of it for not another second. If you are wondering why, I'd like to suggest you already know the reasons; they are many and varied and involve things in our insides we don't have proper nouns for. In which case, I don't need to tell you anything at all.

RM: A SLIDESHOW

(Click.)

"It is impossible to say that New York would have been a better city if Robert Moses had never lived. It is possible to say only that it would have been a different city."
                    —Robert A. Caro, *The Power Broker*, 1975

(Click.)

Overhead view of present-day New York, looking south-southeast toward Queens, Brooklyn, and the Battery, aloft over the Bronx (partial view).

(Click.)

Yale Swimming Team, 1907–1908.

There are fourteen boys. Those in the front row sit in chairs while the others stand—staggered—in two rows at the back. They wear actual swimsuits. A swimsuit for men in 1907–1908 is a pair of very short shorts and a kind of tanktop. These tanktops say: SYA—Yale Swimming Association. It's just like that, too: a small upper-case *s*, a large upper-case *y*, and a small upper-case *a*, all in white block letters. Emphasis on the *Yale*, it seems. Robert Moses stands back row, center. He's the photograph's focal point, its anchor. You can't not look at him. The left side of his face is obscured in shadow. All the other boys are well-lit and pale and looking very much as if they'd rather be somewhere else. Moses looks this way too, sort of. He glowers, appears pissed off. His face's angles cut hard and sharp where the other boys' are soft and doughy. This is the earliest known photograph of Moses. Even his remaining relatives don't have any pictures of him as a child. It's as if he just sprung up out of the ground one day in New Haven, Connecticut, fully-formed. The effect of his position and the light on his face from off camera-left makes him appear foreshortened, as if he's somehow farther away than the rest of the boys. He probably is, actually. He probably is.

(Click.)

Astoria Pool, Astoria, Queens, c. 1981 (Moses not present).

(Click.)

List of positions held by Robert Moses.

Chairman, New York State Council of Parks, 1924–1963
President, Long Island State Parks Commission, 1924–1963
Secretary of State, New York State, 1927–1928
President, Jones Beach Parkway Authority, 1933–1963
President, Bethpage State Park Authority, 1933–1963
Chairman, Emergency Public Works Commission, 1933–1934
Commissioner, New York City Department of Parks, 1934–1960
Chairman, Triborough Bridge and Tunnel Authority, 1934–1981
New York City Planning Commissioner, 1946–1960
Chairman, New York State Power Authority, 1954–1962
President, New York World's Fair, 1960–1966
Special Advisor to the Governor of New York State on Housing, 1974–1975

(Click.)

New York City Department of Parks and Recreation logo mounted on brick pillar, Gotham Plaza, Flushing Meadows, Queens. The Department, which was formed in 1976 without Moses' involvement, is the modern equivalent of the New York City Department of Parks, which Moses ran for a quarter of a century.

(Click.)

A Dream.

Moses finds himself in City Hall in a white suit with pinstripes. He
is approximately the size and shape of a skyscraper. All the other
men in the room are about the size of Matchbox cars. Moses stands
at the podium and booms out his plans for the city: NEW HIGH-
WAYS AND EXPANSIONS OF HIGHWAYS! NEW PARKS AND
PARKWAYS! NEW PLAYGROUNDS AND BRIDGES AND TUN-
NELS! MORE PUBLIC WORKS, PEOPLE! IT'S VITAL TO THE
GROWTH OF THE CITY! The Yes Men, "Yes!" The Councilmen,
"Hear, hear!" Moses hears them but doesn't actually hear them.
There's a buzz in his ear like static, the hum of an electrical plant.
Mayor La Guardia sits at a table to Moses' right; he is also the size
of a Matchbox car. Even the cars outside City Hall, the taxis and
buses and freight trucks: Matchbox cars all. Later, after he's finished
his speech to the board, Moses reaches up and punches an enor-
mous hole in the ceiling of City Hall. He steps out of the building
and into the intersection of Broadway and Murray Street. He roars,
turns into a gorilla, declares himself "KING OF NEW YORK!" in
a kind of gorilla-English and beats his fists upon his chest. Nobody
understands anything he's saying. Moses looks down, sees what
looks to him like a miniature, wheelchaired FDR. There are other
Public Officials in the streets, but none of them stand out to him
like FDR. The citizens of New York who are unfortunate enough
to be in Lower Manhattan just now are running from Moses in all
directions. There's screaming and the holding of hands to faces.
Traffic is gridlocked and everywhere the sound of horns caroms off
the city's buildings. Moses reaches down now and picks up FDR.
FDR protests, strikes Moses' gorilla forearms with his miniature
fists, shouts that "[he's] a Roosevelt, for godsakes! A Roosevelt!" but
to no avail: Moses crushes him in the palm of his hand and tosses
him back to the frantic scene below. After this, he turns, sets his
sights uptown for Gracie Mansion. He's walked this route before,
in the old days with Al Smith: six miles up 3rd Avenue. He crushes

buildings as he goes, calculates construction projects to build on the now-damaged property, contemplates the nature of fine city living, feels the cockles of his heart warm. This is a good dream for Moses. This is a good dream.

(Click.)

Biblical Moses (date unknown).

(Click.)

Moses: Apicoris?

"'Moses didn't say, "I'm a Jew and I'm proud of it," as he should have,' recalls Paul Windels. 'Instead, he said, "It's nobody's business what my religion is." And that got a lot of people very angry.' [...] [I]n shabby *shuls* in the Bronx as well as at Temple Emanu-El, Robert Moses was being called by a term which comes close to being the ultimate insult among pious Jews. Moses, they said, was an *apicoris*, 'a man who says he isn't what he is.'"

—Robert A. Caro, *The Power Broker*, 1975

(Click.)

A dreidel on its side (not Moses').

(Click.)

Franklin Delano Roosevelt dedicating Jones Beach State Park, 1929.

Franklin Delano Roosevelt is not quite FDR here. He's standing, for one thing, and his election as the 32nd US President is four years off. He stands behind a podium in the photograph's center. It looks as if the photographer's caught him in the middle of a word because his mouth is slightly agape. A striped canvas tent seems to be the photograph's backdrop. It lightens things, puts the emphasis on Roosevelt. If you look carefully, though, you can see that almost no one in the photograph is looking at him. Al Smith sits behind him and to his right and is exhaling smoke from a cigar. A woman in a white hat sitting next to Smith looks off camera-left. Several suited men behind Smith are looking at something or someone camera-right. One man—sitting camera-right—wears a tuxedo. He stares intently at the back of Roosevelt's head. The man's face looks bloated somehow, as if he's holding his breath underwater, waiting to come up for air. This is Robert Moses. Everyone camera-left—the ones who look at something or someone camera-right and not at Roosevelt—is probably looking at Moses, it turns out. Jones Beach State Park: this was Moses' baby. It cost more to build than any park anywhere in the world at that point. It brought the city's inhabitants out to Long Island, gave them reprieve from summer's sweltering heat inside the waterless grid. True story: the land Moses needed to build roads to make Jones Beach accessible had been owned for many years by Long Island's 19th-century robber barons. When they heard about Moses' plan for Jones Beach, the robber barons banded together and refused to give up their land—especially if it was going to be used to bring vulgar city folk out their way. One day, Moses had his driver take him out to one of the robber baron's estates where present-day Southern State Parkway runs. He entered the house and waited inside for the robber baron to come home. When at last he arrived, Moses raised his shotgun, pointed it at the wall beside the door the robber baron had just entered, fired it, and said, "You'll give me my land, goddamit. There's plenty more where that came from." Then, quietly, he walked out of the estate past the smoking hole in the wall.

(Click.)

FDR as president, c. 1940.

(Click.)

Moses on FDR.

"Who?"

(Click.)

An air traffic control tower, LaGuardia Airport, Queens, c. 2005.

(Click.)

Moses and Fiorello H. La Guardia, Mayor of the City of New York,
1934–1945.

In City Hall, behind La Guardia's desk. La Guardia looks almost
like a cross between Humpty Dumpty and Santa Claus, except that
he is suited and definitely beardless. He's big-faced and big-bellied
and wears his pants in that over-the-bellybutton way men used to
wear pants in the '30s and '40s. Suspenders and such. His tie is far
too short, and this has the effect of infantilizing the man. He looks
happy for the most part, jolly even. And why shouldn't he be? La
Guardia is widely regarded as the greatest Mayor the City of New
York has ever had. He was the one who finally got the city a commercial airport, he who refused to believe people flying to New York
should have to land in Newark, New Jersey of all places, he who
famously proclaimed as he walked up the steps of City Hall on his
first day of work, "*È finita la cuccagna!*"—"No more free lunch!"—
a reference to his campaign promise to rid city government of the
graft and corruption of the Irish Tammany Hall days. Here, Moses
stands behind and to the left of La Guardia. They're both smiling
widely in a way that doesn't seem put-on for the camera. Moses
wears a white suit. His right hand is on La Guardia's right shoulder.
He seems to be guiding him almost, treating him like a little brother
perhaps. Indeed: Moses towers over the Mayor—a good foot-and-a-
half above. It's uncertain when this picture was taken, but the cut of
their faces and their respective hairlines suggests it's close to 1940.
On December 2nd, 1939, the first commercial flight took off from
New York Municipal Airport (it would later be renamed LaGuardia Airport). The very idea of air travel exhilarated the public, and
even those who couldn't afford to fly flocked to Queens to sit in the
airport and watch the planes take off and land. It only cost a dime.
The subway still cost a nickel at the time. It's interesting to note
that although La Guardia and Moses had little in common on the
surface, both believed they were, above all else, Men of the People.
La Guardia spoke seven languages and used this to his advantage

throughout his campaigns. He could talk to you in your language people said, and this really struck home. For his own part, Moses took no pay from any City position he ever held—all of which positions were appointed or created, sometimes by Moses himself— which made it fairly easy for him to claim he worked only for the people, free of political maneuvering. One has to wonder, then, how La Guardia could have decided to go ahead with Moses' plan for the building of New York Municipal when that plan strictly forbade the building of any subway or rail lines to and from the airport.

> Q: In a city of roughly 7,000,000 in 1939—most of
>   whom did not own a car—how did La Guardia
>   expect the masses, both then and in the future,
>   to have convenient access to air travel?
> A: He didn't. He was merely the Mayor, after all.

(Click.)

Jones Beach State Park water tower, Wantagh, NY (date unknown).

(Click.)

Various women on Moses (qtd. in Caro's The Power Broker, *1975):*

Justice Florence Shientag (friend)
"'He must've been a wonderful lover. He's so direct. No underlying doubts…'"

Hilda Hellman (Moses' cousin)
"'[He was] almost larger than life.'"

Joan Ganz Cooney (one-time producer of Sesame Street)
"'[A]fter I had spent the evening with him [in conversation] I was in love with him.'"[14]

Emily Sims Marconnier (Moses' sister-in-law)
"'He loved to cook. No matter how early I got up, Robert would be in the kitchen and he'd like to know what I'd have—bacon or eggs or whatever.'"

Justice Shientag (on Moses and Moses' wife, Mary, c. 1936)
"'She was a moon whose light was growing less and less. He was going on, a sun, getting brighter and brighter.'"

---

14. Mrs. Cooney was twenty-four at the time—a mere forty years Moses' junior.

(Click.)

Present-day Washington Square Park (not built by Moses) in the Village, Manhattan.

(Click.)

Jane Jacobs on Moses and city expressways.

"Theoretically, city expressways are always presented as means for taking cars off of other streets, and thereby relieving city streets of traffic. In real life, this works only if and when the expressways are well under capacity use; left unconsidered is the eventual destination, off the expressway, of that increased flow of vehicles. Instead of serving as bypassers, expressways in cities serve too frequently as dumpers. Mr. Moses' plan for a downtown expressway in Manhattan, for instance—the one with repercussions on Washington Square—is always presented appealingly as a fast route between the East River bridges and the Hudson River tunnels to keep through traffic out of the city. And yet the actual plan for it includes a spaghetti-dish of ramps into the city. It will be a dumper, and by thus accommodating traffic aimed for the heart of the city, it will actually tend to choke up, instead of aid, city bypass traffic."
    —*The Death and Life of Great American Cities*, 1961

(Click.)

Spaghetti dish (not Moses' or Jacobs').

(Click.)

Moses on the proposed Lower Manhattan Expressway (never built).

"There is nobody against this. Nobody, nobody, nobody but a bunch of, a bunch of mothers."

(Click.)

Moses and family on Luna Island, Niagara Falls, NY. An unknown man approaches the family from camera left. Moses and Moses' mother, Bella, stand at the end of the pedestrian bridge. Moses' older brother Paul, off on his own, stands in the bridge's center (or Moses stands in the bridge's center, off on his own, and Paul stands next to their mother) (date unknown).

(Click.)

Paul Moses on "Mr. Robert".

"Of course he's had an influence. No one's saying he hasn't had an influence. Take a look at the landscape. Almost everything you see, almost every public work in this city is Mr. Robert's. Orchard Beach and Van Cortlandt Park and the Bronx Park and Crotona. Inwood Hill and Highbridge and Riverside Park and the Central Park Zoo and Corlears Hook and Battery Park. All those parks on Long Island he did for the Park Commission. Jones Beach and Fire Island. All those parkways. The Moshulu, the Hutchinson, the Saw Mill River, the Sprain Brook. The Cross County and the Grand Central and the Belt and the Laurelton. The Northern and Southern States. The Wantagh. Those little planned communities: Stuyvesant Town and Peter Cooper Village and Co-op City in the Bronx. The World's Fair, for godsake. Shea Stadium. Something like 700 playgrounds. He built the UN building, and all those bridges: the Verrazano and the Throgs Neck and the Marine; the Henry Hudson, the Cross Bay, and the Whitestone. He built the Brooklyn-Battery Tunnel. All of those expressways: Major Deegan; Van Wyck; Sheridan; Bruckner; Gowanus; Prospect; Whitestone; Clearview. The Cross Bronx. The B.Q.E. The Long Island Expressway. Harlem River Drive. The West Side Highway. You don't need to tell me these things."

(Click.)

The Unisphere in Flushing Meadows (present-day). "Built and pre-sented by the United States Steel Corporation" for the 1964–1965 New York World's Fair to "symbol[ize] [man's] achievements in an expanding universe," the Unisphere is now perhaps best remembered as the object spectacularly destroyed in the 1997 Will Smith-Tommy Lee Jones vehicle, Men In Black.

(Click.)

Moses on Getting Things Done (qtd. in Caro's The Power Broker, *1975):*

"You can't make an omelet without breaking eggs."

"If the end doesn't justify the means, what does?"

"As long as you're on the side of parks, you're on the side of the angels. You can't lose."

(Click.)

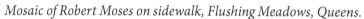

Mosaic of Robert Moses on sidewalk, Flushing Meadows, Queens.

(Click.)

Yale Senior Council, 1909.

There are seven men—boys, really. Six wear dark suits and one wears tweed. The tweed is a bookend. Moses is the tweed. All the boys look much older than they probably are. The slick hair. The skin pale. The hands folded neatly in laps. The air of gentility, aristocracy. These are the people who govern. There are six neckties and one bowtie. Moses sits far left. He leans away from the rest of them. He is darker somehow—like maybe the light hits him differently. He is other, he is other. He sits differently too: one foot forward—farther forward than anyone else's—and one foot back up against the chair's leg. Rounded collars on the shirt. The suit jacket unbuttoned. The manner relaxed. He slouches just a little. The way the boys are arranged makes it look as if Moses is sitting just outside the circle— as if he's an x, y coordinate running tangent to the circle's curve. His face is the only one that looks straight into the camera. The others are cocked slightly up or down, slightly left or right. All the other boys seem to float, their dark suits seeming somehow coterminous with the photograph's curtained backdrop. He looks like he knows something, Moses does. His ears are too large. He smirks, perhaps. He looks like he knows.

END.

ℵO; OR THE STORY OF ISAAC AND HIS MOTHER

{1. My mother was the kind of woman who never liked to show her feelings. 2. People who knew her said she was, above all other things, kind, but that if you didn't know her, or if you'd just met her, you'd think she was cold and distant and heartless, because she'd never touch you, would never hug you or kiss you or even shake your hand. 3. Instead, she'd just nod, look you squarely in the eye and nod. 4. She even did this with me, her own son—especially after the death of my father. 5. My father died when I was 7 in a car wreck outside LaGuardia. 6. His car flipped over several times and his head was crushed and neck broken, and I wasn't even allowed to see his body at the funeral. 7. After his death, mom stopped talking about him completely. 8. I'd bring him up at dinner or when something reminded me of him, but mom would just sit there eating or knitting or filling in the squares of her crossword, silent. 9. I've never faulted mom for this; even then I understood it was just her way of dealing with the grief. 10. My own way of dealing with the grief was different. 11. At night I'd go up onto our roof and watch the planes taking off and landing at LaGuardia. 12. In the same way that I never faulted mom for her silence, she never faulted me for my plane-watching. 13. Even though she knew I probably shouldn't have been climbing up on the roof at such a young age, she understood that this was my way of dealing with the grief, and that if she wanted to be left alone she'd better just go ahead and leave me alone as well. **14.** About a year after my father died, mom started dealing with her grief in a different way: she started reading. **15.** She'd read before, of course, but she hadn't read like this. **16.** This was Serious Reading—directed, purposeful, "Please leave me alone" reading. **17.** She read all the great Holy Books: Confucius' *Analects*; the *Bhagavad Gita*; the *Qur'an*; the *Old* and *New Testaments*; the *Sefer Ha-Bahir*; the *Talmud*; the *Tao Te Ching*; the *Upanishads*; the *Vedas*. **18.** None of them gave her any comfort. **19.** She tried reading them again—straight through from start to finish, again—only this time with a pencil so she could take notes. **20.** Meanwhile, I was growing up. **21.** I'd stopped watching planes at night and had started, in my own way, a Serious schedule of Reading. **22.** Where mom read the Holy Books, I found I had an interest in math. **23.** This was when I was 12, and in the 6th grade at I.S. 230 in Queens. **24.** Through no fault of her own, the math my teacher Mrs. White had us doing was all of a sudden far too easy for me. **25.** It just made sense in a way that nothing had made sense before. **26.** I never got below 100 on any of our tests, and one day after class, Mrs. White took me aside and asked if I'd like to do something a little more challenging. **27.** I said that I would. **28.** She said she would enter me in something called the Continental Math League, and that starting next week I'd have sets of much more difficult and challenging problems to tackle, and that every couple months or so there would be a test that students from all over the country took at the same time, and that the more problems you finished correctly, the more points you got, and at the end of the year the student with the most points won a trophy. **29**. I won the trophy that year and upon winning decided, definitively, that I would become a mathematician. **30**. Mrs. White was thrilled with this, but since our school was poor and mom and I were poor, there was little I could do but keep winning Continental Math League trophies and keep attending my regularly scheduled math classes at I.S. 230. **31**. I would have been resigned to this if I hadn't found myself on a train one day that got rerouted so many times I didn't know where I was or where I was going. **32**. When one is on a train that gets rerouted several times and one is 12 years old, one's best course of action is to get off that train and look at a map. **33**. I did this at the 116th St-Columbia University stop on the 1 line. **34**. Since I'd never been to Columbia University, I decided I'd go aboveground and wander around a little while. **35**. I was extremely tall for my age. **36**. I also had a beard already. **37**. As I wandered around I realized that nobody seemed to pay any attention to the fact that here was a 12-year-old boy all by himself on the campus of a college university. **38**. It was then that I realized I could use this to my advantage. **39**. People thought I was a college student, so why shouldn't I be a college student? **40**. I started attending afternoon lectures in the math building after my classes at I.S. 230 let out. **41**. I'd get the 7 train at 74th St and Roosevelt Av and take it into Times Square, where I'd have to transfer to the 1 going uptown to Columbia. **42**. When I'd get there, I could just sit down in the back of the lecture halls and take notes and get an education for free. **43**. I did this for 5 years, and by the age of 17 I had finite math under my belt and I'd started to become terribly interested in transfinite numbers and the work of Georg Cantor. **44**. If you're not familiar with the work of

Georg Cantor, I'll give you a brief explication: Georg Ferdinand Lud-
wig Philipp Cantor → b. 3/3/1845, St. Petersburg, Russia-d. 1/6/1918,
Halle, Germany; best known as the creator of set theory, with perhaps
his primary contribution being the establishment of the importance
of 1-to-1 correspondence between sets, and the discovery that there
are, in all likelihood, an "infinity of infinities." **45.** The specifics of
Cantor's work are neither here nor there, but what is both very much
here and there is the fact that I became obsessed with G. F. L. P. Cantor—addicted to him, you might say. **46.** Now what about my mother,
then?—what was going on with her? **47.** Well, there is a parallel here,
of course: mom's absorption in the Holy Books had continued all this
time (it continued for the rest of her life, in fact), and it paralleled my
own absorption in the work of Cantor and set theory and ∞. **48.** In
fact, most afternoons during that year I found Cantor, mom and
myself represented a kind of physical 1-to-1 correspondence: she
upstairs at her desk with a Holy Book open and a pencil in hand, her
back arched, her head held just above the text, her eyes focused and
moving in penitent rectilinear beauty over the words of the gods as
the sun shone in her window, a woman alone with her soul‖myself
just one floor below her, sitting at my own desk with my own math-
ematics book open, my own pencil in hand, my own back arched and
my own head held just above the text, my own eyes focused and
moving back and forth and back in a kind of ∞-like motion between
Cantor's words and symbols and my own attempts to understand the
universe that I scribbled in salt-and-pepper notebook after salt-and-
pepper notebook, a boy alone with his soul. **49.** No understanding of
the universe was reached by the end of that summer, though. **50.**
Mom finished her 6th go-through of the Holy Books and still felt

unfulfilled, and I couldn't quite grasp what G. F. L. P. Cantor was getting at before he went supposedly mad and died unrecognized and unfulfilled in a sanatorium. **51.** Nevertheless, I was still determined to be a mathematician, and it was with great excitement and anxiety that I packed my bags and nodded my mom goodbye on the steps of our row house on 76th Street in Jackson Heights, bound for Columbia University where I was to study math for real this time. **52.** This excitement was short-lived, though. **53.** 2 months into my 1st semester, mom got cancer and I had to come back home to watch over her. **54.** She apologized every day and said that she was sorry she couldn't give me the kind of life my father wanted for me. **55.** It was the 1st time she had voluntarily spoken of him since he died when I was 7. **56.** I said I understood and read to her from whatever Holy Book she wanted me to read from. **57.** She stayed in bed almost all the time. **58.** I remember the 1st time I had to help her to the bathroom that 1st day I came home. **59.** It was the 1st time she'd let me touch her that I could remember. **60.** Her skin felt dry and brittle and scratchy, not unlike the pages of the books I was reading to her. **61.** I cried for the 1st time in my life. **62.** She started to speak of my father more often. **63.** I said I missed him. **64.** She said she missed him more than anything in the world. **65.** I said what did my father do? because I couldn't remember. **66.** She said my father always wanted to be an architect but that he'd had to settle for teaching woodshop and technology to middle-schoolers in Jackson Heights. **67.** I cried for the 2nd time in my life. **68.** That night I went into the basement and looked at my father's tools and wondered where he might be if he was anywhere and about the possibilities and implications of oblivion. **69.** The next morning I asked mom why she wasn't getting any chemo. **70.** She said the cancer wasn't benign and that chemo would only draw things out—only make them more painful—and there was already enough pain in the world as it was anyway, wasn't there, Isaac? **71**. As she said this, I could see her hair was falling out without the chemo and that earlier that morning she must've been crying. **72**. Mom died shortly thereafter, and I cried for the 3rd time in my life. **73**. After the funeral I had a very hard time readjusting to the world. **74**. I sat at mom's desk every day and thought about how long and how conscientiously she had sat there, day after day after the death of my father, searching for meaning in all the cultures of the world. **75**. A week passed... then another. **76**. I tried to pick up my math books again but for some reason they seemed cold and distant and heartless—just symbols on a page rather than descriptions of a recognizable world. **77**. I planted some tomatoes in the little garden behind our row house, and as I did this I thought, The sun feels like the moon, and the moon feels like the sun. **78**. I tried living like this for a week: sleeping during the day and living during the night. **79**. I switched back for a week, but switched back again when I realized there wasn't really any difference. **80**. That is to say: if I slept at night and lived in the day or slept during the day and lived at night, it didn't seem to matter at all. **81**. My life went on like this indefinitely. **82**. In fact, it might very well still be going on like this. **83**. At this point I don't feel I'm at liberty to discuss what is real and what is unreal. **84**. I do know that there came a time when I started reading mom's books without mom. **85**. At 1st I saw them in a different light. **86**. I'm not sure why, because I'd read them all before. **87**. Perhaps I hadn't been paying attention though; perhaps I'd only mouthed the words to mom as she lay dying in her bed. **88**. Either way, the words began to have some meaning for me as I read them to myself. **89.** Each one seemed distinct and new, and when I got through them all a 1st time, I immediately read them through again, this time with a pencil in hand so I could take notes. **90.** Do I have to say what happened after this?—do I have to say how things changed and how I'm all confused again? **91.** I suppose I will. **92.** I suppose I will. **93.** I suppose I will. **94.** My 3rd time through the Holy Books was what did it. **95.** I'd sit there at my mother's desk sure that I was reading one thing, sure the whole time through, sure that this right here, this thing I'm reading right in front of me, this thing is the *Qur'an.* **96.** But then when it was time to quit and go to bed, I'd close the book and see that it was not the *Qur'an* after all, it was the *Talmud* or it was the *Old Testament* or it was the *Sefer Ha-Bahir.* **97.** It doesn't matter in the end because they all became the same to me. **98.** And I would sit there feeling enlightened and confused, and wondering what was real. **99.** And then I'd get to thinking that perhaps it didn't matter, perhaps enlightenment and confusion was the same thing too... or maybe they were something else, I don't know. **100.** Either way, the only thing I'd end up doing was sitting alone asking questions to myself, thinking, What if they're the same, what if they are different, what if they're the same, what if they are different, what if dad had lived, what if they are different, what if mom had lived, what if they are different, what if god is Cantor, what if they are different, what if Cantor's god, what if they are different, what if math's religion, what if they are different, what if dad had lived, what if they are different, what if I am real, what if there's a difference, what if I'm unreal, what if I am different, what if they're the same, what if they are different, what if they're the same, what if they are different? ... }[1]

---

1. I am not sure if I'm still doing this today.

Quartet (2)

It's 1892, Chicago, Illinois. A man leaves his job at an advertising agency one evening and is struck by some sort of daydream in which he imagines a little girl imagining herself transplanted to an archetypal land of Good and Evil, a land with witches and strange *Alice's Adventures in Wonderland*-type characters and a mysterious Overlord who's both seemingly unattainable and omniscient and, perhaps, a total hoax. The man's most prominent feature is a thick, black mustache. His hair is parted hard down the middle and combed back flat against his skull. Standing there outside his advertising agency's building—hat actually in hand because of the Windy City's famous wind—the man is epiphanically convinced this vision will be his saving grace. It will overshadow all his past failures, and he will, eventually, be world-renowned for the creative output that comes from this particular daydream. No longer will it matter that his parents think he's feminine and weak. Nor, for that matter, will his failed poultry business and theater career be of any consequence. His frequent bankruptcy will be forgotten, as will his failed grocery store and failed local newspaper. He may even be able to quit both his current jobs—the one just mentioned hereabove and the one he has as a fact-checker at the Chicago *Evening Post*. He will get his due. He will have his comeuppance. He will etc., etc., etc.

Not just yet, though. Instead, what happens is the man's life stays very much the same for the next three years. The only notable difference comes in the form of a book. This book is not a book that contains stories of his own: it's a book in which he writes—re-writes—prose versions of Mother Goose rhymes. The book is moderately successful, but the situation is such that the man puts little stock in this success, because he knows everyone knows the book does not include work that is his own, so to speak. Yes, it is his work in the sense that he is the one who put those words in that particular order, but he did not come up with the characters and the situations, and to his understanding of things this means the work is not his own. It's not original, and since it is the man's great ambition to be successful by way of originality, he is not satisfied with his Mother Goose success. He begins to sink into melancholy. The only thing that keeps him going—apart from his desire to be a good husband and father—is his faith in the importance of his 1892 vision. Most nights, when his wife and kids are asleep, he trudges down the hallway of their Chicago apartment to the kitchen and tries to put his daydream into words. Nothing ever seems to work, though. He writes and writes, and tosses out and tosses out. This, too, starts to seem like just another failure.

One day, about a year later, things start to change for the man. He has the daydream again and realizes immediately what he's been neglecting in all his previous efforts to get the daydream down. It's the Overlord—he'd forgotten about the Overlord. He'd remembered the little girl and her three companions, and he'd remembered that she'd been imagining imagining herself in another world, and he'd even remembered the witches. But the Overlord he'd left out. And now that he'd remembered it, he knew how to write the tale. The Overlord was the most important part: he was the thing after which the little girl and her companions sought. He was the mysterious element, the God of her little imagined world, the string-puller, the setter-in-motion, the impetus, the cause that renders effect.

Something's still kind of off, though. Yes, the man is correct in thinking he's figured out that the Overlord is the key to the writing of this tale, but he hasn't at this point remembered that in his original daydream the Overlord is not really an Overlord at all. He's a fraud, a hoax, a nice man from Omaha, Nebraska who finds himself the object of worship of the people of a foreign land he happens upon by accident.

This is the real key to the story, and it's only years later that he sees this, rectifies his error, and does in fact gain almost immediate and ever-lasting fame. Of course, as is often the case in tales like this,[15] the man fails to see the true import of his story. He's blinded by fame and fortune—which he repeatedly gains and loses, by the way, due to an absolutely terrible sense of business—and he writes his story endlessly, penning sequel after sequel until the day he dies of a stroke at the age of 65.

His story is still being told today. Many followers of the man's work have taken it upon themselves to continue telling in various mediums the story of the little girl and her three friends and the witches and the Overlord. There have been film adaptations and stage adaptations, impromptu online streaming videos, and live performances in parks. In fact, the man's story is such an entrenched part of the current cultural lexicon it's probably no good for me to

---

15. That is to say, tales of ambition with respect to fame.

be speaking of it in such indirect terms. I'll just come right out and say it: every version of the story—including its original iteration—has missed the point. The focus seems always to be on the little girl's experience, and on the battle between the forces of Good and Evil. This is not surprising, as all the iterations of the story—or at least those with which most of us are familiar—present the Good vs. Evil theme in a wildly entertaining way. We enjoy it when the evil witch is defeated and she withers away; we rejoice when the little girl is no longer frightened and her three friends are no longer suffering from their respective conditions. Yes; this is all true. The important point that's embedded in this story, though, is that the Overlord—the nice man from Omaha, Nebraska—is not an Overlord at all. Furthermore, he's utterly unnecessary to the little girl and her three friends. He lives in a house of cards, and all it takes to realize this is for the little girl to be either unafraid or for her to wake herself up—which of course amounts to the same thing. Given the constant state of flux and disorder in the world today, especially among this world's heads of states and governments, and given the uncertainty of so many different aspects of modern life, what better lesson to consider than this: the Overlord is a hoax, and all one might need to make things better is to be unafraid to reveal their usurping master?

Walts waltz

—I'm looking it up right now, Dad. Dad, I'm looking it up. Don't come down.

—Hold on, I'm coming down.

—No, stay there! I'm looking it up! Just stay there, okay?

—All right. So look it up.

—That's what I'm doing.

—I'll just stay here, then.

—Good.

—*Here* is out of the bathroom and at the top of the stairs now, in case you're wondering. I'm sitting here at the top of the stairs waiting to hear what you find.

—

—

—

—So, what's it say?

—I don't know yet.

—You mean it's not in there? You can't find it?

—No, I don't *know* yet.

—What are you in? *Merriam-Webster* or *American Heritage*?

—Dad, I don't know if it's not there because I'm not there yet, okay? I'm looking. Can you just hold on?

—I'm holding on. I was just curious what you were in is all.

—Keep holding then, okay?

—Roger that, kid. Keep holding.

—

—

—

—I've got Barbasol all over my face and a razor in my hand, in case you're interested.

—

—No?

—

—Well, you know what? While you're finding that I'm gonna go put the razor down and wipe this stuff off my face, all right? Just yell it out when you find it.

—

—

—

—

—

—Update: back at the top of the stairs. Barbasol wiped off face. Razor sitting securely in its razor-holder. Can you give me an update now?

—I've almost got it, I think

—Do you want me to come down there and help you out? I can come down there and help you out.

—Dad, I can do it. Just hold on.

—No, you're right. We should just keep yelling up and down the stairs. How often do we get to yell up and down the stairs? We're men, right? When your mother's out we should communicate only by way of yelling, I think. What do you say? I think Ezra could get behind that.

—

—

—

—Where is your mother, by the way?

—I've got it.

—You've got it?

—No, wait.

—How are you spelling it?

—I'm not spelling it wrong. It's here. Or here. I've got it. Yeah, I've got it now.

—What's it say?

—Well, for one thing it *is* supposed to start with a *U*, and not an *O* and then a *U*, like you said. That's why I couldn't find it. *You* were spelling it wrong.

—Is that right? That's strange. I almost always see it with an *O* and then a *U*. Not that I see it all that often. What else does it say?

—It says it's the symbol, usually in the form of a circle, of a snake or dragon eating its tail.

—A snake or *dragon* eating its tail?

—Yeah, a snake or dragon eating its tail.

—Interesting. I would have thought a snake or serpent eating its tail, but I guess dragon's fine. Which did you say you were in? *Merriam-Webster*?

—I didn't say. But yes, *Merriam-Webster*.

—Well, all right then. There you go.

—What do you mean there I go?

—I mean there you go. Now you know what it means. Now you know what it means and I can go back to shaving.

—Yeah, I know what it means but why do you think he'd call me that? It doesn't even make any sense, right?

—Well, I don't know. Why do *you* think he'd call you that?

—I don't know. It seems like a bad thing to call me though, doesn't it?

—I suppose it does.

—It doesn't make any sense.

—Remember that one time he convinced you Zimbabwe was a swear word? That didn't make any sense either.

—Yeah.

—

—

—Hey, you know what? Never mind about the yelling all of a sudden, all right? Why don't you just come in here and sit next to me at the top of the stairs—or at least come to the bottom of the stairs so I can see you while we talk, all right?

—Okay.

—

—

—

—

—Good. Now. Tell me again what happened.

—We were just shooting the ball around at first, just me and Ezra. But then these two kids we played against last week showed up and we played them two-on-two for a while. We did that, and then we came home, and then he called me an eff-ing uroboros and charley-horsed me, and then he walked out the door.

 —Hmm. Right. Is that all? Were you winning at the park?

 —We won one.

 —Okay, okay. Which of course means you lost some too, then, yes?

 —Yeah, we lost some.

 —How many'd you lose?

 —I don't know. Three, I think? Four? We lost four.

 —So you won one and lost four.

 —Yeah.

 —Well, there's that.

 —

 —How would you say Ezra was on the way home? How did he act?

 —You mean besides calling me an eff-ing uroboros and charley-horsing me, how did he act?

 —Sure, but those too. The whole time, really. Say from the end of the last game to the time he walked out the door after you'd gotten back home. How would you say he *was*?

 —I mean, I don't know. He was Ezra. I guess he seemed angry.

 —Angry. Okay. Now, judging on a scale of one to ten—one being Ezra when he has to do dishes, let's say, and ten being Ezra when he and your mother talk about Reagan—what would you say was his level of anger on the way home?

 —I don't know. I'd say four, maybe? Maybe four?

 —Did he talk to you on the train?

 —He was reading on the train.

—Okay, fine: he was reading on the train. But did he talk to you at all? When you came aboveground did he walk with you, or did he do the thing he does where he walks at least a couple of feet in front of you and won't let you really catch up?

—He walked in front of me, I guess. I never caught up.

—Right. Well then just based on what you've told me it sounds like he was maybe more like a seven or an eight on the Ezra Scale of Anger.

—A seven or an *eight*?

—A seven or an eight, yes. Which means he won't be talking to you for about three days, I'm guessing.

—We have the same room.

—And it'll be a quiet room at that.

—What do I do, though? I mean I don't get why he's so mad at me.

—You just wait it out, is what you do. He'll get over it. He's like your mother: he's got this temper he doesn't really know how to handle.

—Yeah, but you don't have to share a room with him.

—Plus, the midterm elections are coming up. He'll forget about this whole thing even by the end of the week. Just watch.

—

—

—

—You don't look satisfied. I haven't done my fatherly duty here, have I?

—I'm *not* satisfied. How can I be satisfied? I just don't see why he's so mad if he's just gonna forget about it by the end of the week.

—I don't know. One and four's not a very good day at the park. And maybe he had something else going on nobody knows about. Maybe it's girls. Does he have a girlfriend these days?

—No. I don't know, it's just that they beat us every time last week. And this week we won one, at least.

—Did they? They beat you *every time* last week?

—Yeah, I couldn't make anything.

—And this week? You were better this week?

—I was good this week, yeah. I was a lot better than he was.

—Hmm. You say you were *a lot* better than he was? Is that what you said?

—Yeah. In the one we won I scored every one of our points, and my guy only scored twice. I thought he'd be happy we won one.

—Hmm.

—Hmm what? What's all this hmm?

—

—

—

—Dad! What's all this *hmm*?

—Well, here's what's all this hmm. Your brother doesn't like to lose, a). That's the first thing. But you already know that. The second thing, b), and you may not know this yet, is he hates it when you're better than him at anything. He hates it when anyone's better than him at anything. It's a problem he has. You didn't know this? He gets that face with the pursed lips. This is why he won't play me in chess.

—But I'm not better than him.

—I've seen you play. You're definitely better.

—I'm better?

—You're better. Trust me, you're better. But don't tell him I said that, okay?

—So that's it? He's just mad because he thinks I'm better?

—That's probably not *just* it. That's probably at least some of it, though. He looks at it like this: you're his little brother, he's three years older than you and he wants to see you do well, sure, but what he doesn't want is to see you do well at his expense.

—What do you mean at his expense?

—I mean he wants you to do well but not so well that you do better than he does. It's just a thing he has. Harold has it too, except in that scenario Harold is Ezra and Ezra's you. I have it too. I didn't want Unk to be better than me at anything. Even though I also wanted him to do well at the same time. It's a weird brother thing.

—Do you think I have it?

—Well, I don't really know just yet. We'll have to wait and see. I don't think you do, though. You're more like your mother, where you draw no distinction between who's doing well so long as in the end the team as a whole does well. Does this make sense?

—I guess so. But then what about what he said? That still doesn't make any sense.

—What he said was him just blowing off steam. He was try-ing to impress you in a way, actually. Also a weird brother thing. By using a word you don't even know to insult you in a way you won't be able to understand. It's a lesson in tone, sort of.

—Dad, I don't know what that means.

—Well, all right, how about this: do you know what a Black Hole is? Do they teach you about Black Holes in school?

—I think I know what it is. It's something in space, right?

—Right, it's something in space. It's something in space that swallows stuff and doesn't ever let that stuff come back. More specifically, a Black Hole absorbs all the light that hits it and doesn't reflect any of that light back out into space. I think.

—

—So what I'm telling you, then, is I think Ezra might've thought you were being a little bit of a Black Hole out there on the court today. Meaning he'd pass you the ball and you'd shoot it every time, without ever passing it back.

—I *did* pass it back, though. He just wasn't making anything and I was.

—Even so. To him you weren't passing it back enough, maybe. Ezra's very big on ball movement. I've noticed that about him. He hates zone defense and teams that isolate players instead of running motion offenses and setting downscreens and stuff. That's why he likes the NBA over college and it's why he likes the Celtics instead of the Knicks. Watch how many screens they set for Bird some time. Bernard King gets none of that. He has to create almost all his own shots.

—But he wasn't making anything, Dad. He missed like five layups in a row.

—Nevertheless. That's your brother. That's Ezra.

—I feel kind of bad.

—Well, that was the point, right? He wanted to make you feel bad for a while. But like I said, don't worry. He'll forget about it. It's not gonna be a big deal at all by the end of the week, all right? I promise.

—All right, I guess.

—I'm gonna go finish shaving now, okay? You need anything else?

—No.

—

—

—

—Hey, but what about what he said, though?

—What about what he said. Right. What about what he said, what about what he said…

—

—Well, like I said before, he wanted to make you feel bad for a little while, so obviously he was trying to insult you. But maybe what Ezra doesn't know is that what he said can be something pretty good, too. Maybe he doesn't know that.

—How can it be something pretty good too if he was insulting me?

—Someone really smart a really long time ago talked about it like that. You know Plato? You guys talk about Plato in school?

—No. What'd Plato say about it though?

—Plato said it was kind of better than anything that ever was, actually. That the uroboros was the best thing there was. Because unlike everything else, the uroboros didn't need anything outside itself. And since it was the only thing that existed, since it didn't need anything outside itself, it didn't need to eat or go to the bathroom or anything, because everything it needed was all right there in its insides. It was all already a part of it.

—*Every*thing was already a part of it?

—Everything. The whole world was right there, right inside itself. Everything and anything.

—

—

—Okay, that's good, I guess. But why's it a snake, though?

—Plato talked about that, too. He said that since there was nothing it needed outside itself, since it was all of existence, the form it would take would be a form without any hands or feet.

—Because it didn't need to go anywhere, right? It didn't need hands and feet because it didn't need to go anywhere!

—Right, exactly. It was just a snake, the only thing that was, and the only movement it made was in a circle in the same spot, over and over, so it just went around and around, always swallowing its own tail, and always devouring itself and creating itself at the same time. Now you can bet Ezra didn't know that. You can bet he only thought you'd find out something bad about it.

—And it's not all bad stuff about it.

—Right. Oh, and there's this too: it would never die. It's immortal, Plato said. So how about that? Take *that* Ezra! Am I right or am I right?

—Yeah, I guess that's pretty good.

—What do you mean that's *pretty good*? Of course that's good. It's great!

—Yeah.

—

—

—You're gonna sit here awhile?

—Yeah, I guess. Maybe next time I won't shoot so much, though. Even if I'm not missing and he's not making anything. Maybe that's a good idea.

 —Maybe.

 —Yeah.

 —Yeah.

 —

 —

 —Hey, Dad?

 —Walt.

 —Thanks.

 —Anytime.

Colloquy

I. ANECDOTE OF THE BAR.

Lao Tzu lives in a farmhouse off the old highway. He spends most afternoons lying in the backseat of a broken-down, blue VW Beetle. Three of its tires are flat. Half its hubcaps are missing, and feral grass grows up around its sides. Lao Tzu plays mandolin in the backseat—his father's mandolin. His father lives in the People's Republic of China, and although they've never met, Lao Tzu's seen clipped, sepia-toned images of him on Wikipedia. His father is a poet. He writes haiku and senryū and has published a novel, the title of which is sometimes translated as *Western Eyes*. Lao Tzu's mother thought she was a singer. She left him to follow the Dead and hasn't been back since. Lao Tzu was only six. His maternal grandmother raised him thereafter to be a "good American boy." His public school experience was unremarkable. He was considered a good student, though he was in fact quite average. His college experience was equally unremarkable. Again though, he was considered a good student. Lao Tzu always put this down to his serious face and quiet demeanor. After graduation, he hugged his grandmother and told her he had no plans except to walk south until something seemed good enough to stop for. He left her house in Syracuse, NY and didn't rest for more than a day in any town until he reached the mountains of Tennessee. He told himself that being there felt like remembering something he'd never known. He wrote a letter to his grandmother and rented a P. O. Box for $10 a month. In the letter he asked if she could send him three things: Woody Guthrie's *Bound for Glory*; a blue button-down shirt he'd left in the dryer; his father's mandolin. The package took a week to arrive. Lao Tzu spent the week walking the streets. He did most of his walking at night. There were three saloons on the town's main street, and all three had music. Lao Tzu adopted a rotating schedule for visiting the saloons so he could listen to the local bands and singers. He drank local beer and grew a local beard and wore a BP gas station hat. The bartenders all knew his name. When the package finally arrived, Lao Tzu brought it back to the hotel where he'd been staying. He took out his father's mandolin and practiced all day. Later that night, he went to one of the saloons and asked if he could sit in with the band. The band agreed wholeheartedly. They played into the morning hours, and people ate, drank, and were merry in the way Tennesseans eat, drink, and are merry. Lao Tzu was a hit, and it was agreed upon by all that his mandolin songs sounded more than anything else like the people of Tennessee.

II. BEND OVER BACKWARD.

A very good friend of mine—a woman I've known for quite some time—had one of the most horrific years last year of anyone I've ever heard of, ever. First, she lost her mother and her father to cancer in the same month. Then, two months later, her younger brother was killed driving down the highway when a stray bullet a hunter had shot came through the passenger side window and lodged inside his temple. Understandably, my friend decided to take some time off work. She asked her employer if it'd be all right if she took a couple months to recover, and they of course willingly obliged. At the end of two months, my friend was still in a state of shock and said she didn't feel anywhere near ready enough to go back to work. Her employer balked at this, and several weeks later they ended up firing her, and now my friend's involved in a legal battle over whether her employer had the right to do so. She's also seeing a therapist now two times a week, and she's developed a kind of social anxiety disorder that makes it difficult for her to do simple things like go to the grocery store. I feel so bad for my friend every day I don't know what to do. I get her groceries for her sometimes, and often I even pay for them out of my own pocket. She calls me on the phone almost every night and talks for at least an hour about the way she is feeling. She tells me she's trying to express the pain and fear and dread she feels inside but that she doesn't know how to express it, and I sit there with the phone up to my ear listening, trying not to weep. She herself doesn't often weep. She just keeps calling and telling me about her therapist and how he's not helping, about how much pain she feels she's in and how afraid she feels all the time, about how she thinks she's so completely and utterly changed that she'll never be able to feel things like boredom again, because being bored would mean she's normal and right now she feels anything but normal. She talks and talks and talks, and sometimes, as I'm sitting on the stool in the kitchenette listening to her voice, I have this urge to hang up on her, to just sort of accidentally end the call and pretend it was the phone that disconnected and hung up on her, the phone and not me, her friend. This is awful, I know. She's always saying the same things and never seems to be getting anywhere. I've never done this; I've never hung up on her and probably never will. Every time I think I want to, I hate myself for even having thought of it, because what kind of friend does something like that? Friends listen and say things like "I understand" and "Nobody's been through what you've been through" and "Don't worry about bothering me"—she often feels as if she's bothering me when she talks about these things—"You'd do the same for me if the situations were reversed." All these things are true things, I think. I do understand—to the extent that I understand understanding—and nobody—not anybody—has been through what she's been through. And of course she'd do the same for me if the situations were reversed. These things are true, and for the most part my friend agrees. But she also keeps saying that even though she's appreciative of everything I've done and am doing, and even though she hopes I continue to do these things a friend does—even though I'm doing these things, she says it's not enough, it's not even close to being anywhere near enough. And the things I say and do, they almost always seem to make things *worse* for her, she says. She says instead of comforting her and making her feel as if she's not alone in the world, what I do more often than not is I make her feel more alone than she's ever felt in her life, more grief-stricken, more totally sick and gross inside. Several times now she's asked me how I could possibly say "I understand," how I could just sit there on the other end of the line and say something as senseless and stupid as "I understand" when it's clear I just totally even can't. She cries after she says this, and she apologizes and says she doesn't mean it, but that she also can't help it and hopes I can forgive her. She's also asked me why I'd say something like "Nobody's been through what you've been through," because that too only seems to validate how alone and sick she feels. One day she screamed at me for a good five minutes, told me I was unbelievably insensitive and stupid and that I had no fucking right telling her something like "Nobody's been through what you've been through." She wept like I've never heard anybody weep after this. She apologized profusely and told me I was so good to be so good to her when she was so bad to me. She said she was so so grateful I existed and that she knew me and that I considered her my friend. It's still going on like this now, and honestly I'm not sure how much more of this I can take. It got so bad the other day that she was sobbing before I even picked up the phone and she didn't stop for an hour and then told me she was sorry more times than I can count. Once she settled down, she said something to me I'm still thinking about. She said she'd been thinking about what I'd said a while back about not worrying about bothering me. She told me she felt horrible about this, but that she'd been thinking about it and she wasn't certain she'd be able to do the same for me if the situations were reversed. She said she'd like to think she would, but that now, right now, she couldn't say for sure she would, and that she hated herself for having thought of it. I told her not to worry. I said it was okay and hopefully we wouldn't be in that position anytime soon. After that she said, "Yeah," and I said, "Yeah," and we hung up. I hope things get better for her, I really do. I really, really, really, fucking do.

III. MIMESIS.

—Mom?

 —Yes.

 —I'm thinking about the mime again.

 —Okay.

 —From the movie? The mime from the movie? You remember? Baptiste?

 —I remember, honey. What about him?

 —

 —Honey?

 —I don't know.

 —Well, so what are you thinking about about the mime?

 —I'm thinking…

 —Yes?

 —I think I'm in love with him.

 —

 —

 —You think you're in love with the mime?

 —Yeah.

 —Yes; say, "Yes," honey.

 —Yes.

 —Yes, what?

 —Yes, I think I'm in love with the mime.

 —The mime isn't real, honey.

 —I know. But I still think I'm in love with him.

 —Honey, the mime is an actor.

 —I know that too. But I still think I'm in love with him. I keep watching him up on stage when he's acting and miming, and then watching him backstage when he isn't acting and miming and I just keep thinking I'm in love with him. And then I see how sad he is at the end. You remember? When he's running and he's really sad and lost in the crowd? You remember?

—I remember.

—Well, I just see him and I think that I'm in love with him and that I really want to *be* him.

—You want to be the mime, or you want to be the actor?

—I want to be the mime. But I also think I'm in love with him.

—Honey, he's always acting. Even when he's miming, he's acting. Even when he's backstage and not acting and not miming, he's still acting. He's always acting, honey.

—I know.

—But you still think you're in love with him?

—Yes.

—And you think you'd like to be him?

—Yes.

—

—

—Being in love with him and wanting to be him are different things, you know?

—

—Honey? Did you hear me?

—I heard you.

—And?

—I know.

—You know what?

—I know you're right.

—Okay. How's your homework?

—

—

—Mom?

—Walt.

—Never mind.

LITTLE PRIVATE SYSTEMS

On December 29th, 2004—the day before my 25th birthday—I decided that the two most important things that ever happened in my life happened that past year: first, on August 8th, I took a job as Assistant Curator at the Belfer Audio Laboratory and Archive on the campus of Syracuse University in Syracuse, New York; and second, on December 29th, I discovered an unlabeled TDK D60 High Output Normal Position Dynamic Cassette tape at the back of my late father's desk.

The tape was dusty, and it'd been left by my late father in (what I thought) very strange juxtaposition with the following objects: a small brown glass bottle of Elmer's No-Wrinkle Rubber Cement; two white boxes of unused checks from HSBC rubber-banded together; an unopened VHS tape entitled *Four Wheeler: Ultimate Four Wheeling Video Series: Extreme Four Wheeling: Top Truck Challenge*, featuring four monster trucks of various primary colors driving into and over each other on an attractive slate gray background. The rest of the desk was empty.

My older brother John and I had driven separately to our late parent's house in Macedon the previous weekend and had emptied out the house as best we could, boxing up and keeping the few things we did want, and putting whatever we didn't want out with the trash. I had had to leave early though—Denis, a technician from the Audio Lab, had called me on my cellphone about some missing 78s—and I'd told John just to finish whatever he was working on, that I'd see him sometime soon, and that I'd come back by myself the next weekend to finish my parts of the house. He agreed and kept working, and I went back to Syracuse, thinking only of the missing 78s.

That week is like a blur to me still. I woke up, showered, went to the Lab, worked on some long-untouched Folkways acetates, came home, ate dinner, and went to bed five days straight. Sometimes I try to remember if I thought about the tape on my late father's desk at all that week. Even though I don't think it's possible I didn't think about it, I have no memory of doing so. In fact, I don't even think I thought about the house, or John, or going back to the house, let alone anything inside its rooms.

But home has a way of calling you back without your brain ever having to register it, and at five o'clock that Friday, there I was again, heading west on the New York State Thruway. If you've ever driven on it, you know that the Thruway has a sort of blankness to it. A feeling of almost being erased. I don't know exactly what it is. There's something about the landscape, about the trees and the fields and the straightness of the drive that seems to empty out your head as you move along. As if the simplicity of the drive itself simplifies the driver, makes him childlike. And before you know it you're veering off to the right at some anonymous green exit sign, and slowing to a stop at some anonymous toll booth to hand over some change to an anonymous cashier.

The drive that day must have been no different. In fact, thinking of it now, I can't remember anything about the drive, not even the parts after I exited the Thruway. The first thing I really do remember about that day is standing alone in my late parent's house, over my late father's desk. The rest of the desk, it turns out, was not empty. I found myself standing there looking at something I had never seen before, something that hadn't been there the previous weekend—something other than the rubber cement and the unused checks and the *Four Wheeler* VHS and the dusty TDK Cassette tape. I was looking at an even more dusty and very probably unused Plug-In Lamp & Appliance Timer, Model SB11C, by Intermatic.

I don't know what my late father had intended using the Timer for (and, apparently, neither did he), but I do know that the price tag was still on it. The words and numbers on the tag were a little faded, a little gray. Nevertheless, I could see that the Timer had been purchased for $8.19 at Steven's Hardware in what must have been the late 1980s, because that's when there had been a gas leak in the middle of the night in the Steven's Hardware basement that blew the whole place up.

Yes, that's how it happened.

I remember now because I was sleeping over at my next-door neighbor and best friend Norman McClellan's house. (This was not an uncommon occurrence in those days; my best guess is that I slept at the McClellan's house three or four nights a week, ages eight through eighteen.) Norman's parents and his older brother Andy all had gone to bed, but Norman and I stayed up all night in the upstairs living room, playing a little game we'd invented called Dice Baseball by the light of Norman's father's yellow Eveready flashlight.

Dice Baseball was strictly an offensive game. Each player batted only, and it was easy to play anywhere, because all you needed was a blue Bic round stic pen, an official score sheet, something hard to write on, and three die. Whoever's turn it was to bat rolled the dice for each batter on his team, until, like Real World Baseball, they rolled three outs. The combined sum of the numbers face-up on the die after the roll resulted in some specific Real World Baseball scenario. It took us a while to get the rules just right, but eventually we realized that the middle sums—say, six through fifteen—occurred far more frequently than the extreme high and extreme low sums. And since Norman and I were exceedingly sensible ten-year-old boys, we knew that sums three through five and sums sixteen through eighteen had to correspond with whatever the most infrequent Real World Baseball scenarios were (i.e., home run, triple, hit by a pitch, etc.); and that being given, we also knew that the remaining aforementioned middle sums naturally had to correspond with whatever were the most common Real World Baseball scenarios (i.e., ground out, fly out, single, walk, strikeout, etc.). We would then mark down the roll for each corresponding batter on one of the official score sheets that we made with the help of Norman's Xerox-employed father's massive Xerox copier for the home. (I think this went a long way toward our playing most Dice Baseball games at Norman's house; my late father, being a construction worker on a demo team, did not own a Xerox copier for the home, and also didn't like team sports the way Mr. McClellan did. And one time he threw out a handwritten copy of the rules I'd spent an entire afternoon making.)

But I digress (as the people at the Audio Lab tell me all the time).

That night I was the New York Mets and Norman was the New York Yankees. I remember that he was batting when it happened. I remember because I'd just rolled three consecutive thirteens (three strikeouts, or "Ks") and was furious. I grudgingly handed the dice over to Norman. He took them from me very cautiously and rolled as if he didn't want to roll.

You'll never guess what happened next.

The little bastard rolled the most infrequent roll in all of Dice Baseball: a four—a one, a one, and a two—or, in Real World Baseball terms, a home run.

I can't describe to you how furious this must've made me. I'd like to think it's comparable to when somebody calls the Audio Lab and says, "I'm looking for a recording," and doesn't know the musician's name or the title of the song or the date of the recording, or if the recording is on primary cylinder or disc or magnetic tape. It's totally infuriating, and I think that's probably how I felt sitting on the floor in the McClellan's upstairs living room being beaten by chance.

Of course, it seems silly now; but to my ten-year-old mind the Dice World was the whole world. A loss was like finding out your spouse was cheating on you. It probably didn't help that I was an angry little kid to begin with. Like wall-punching angry, and couch-kicking angry, and heave-the-dinner-plate-across-the-table-at-my-brother angry. I didn't feel guilty about being angry with my family though. It was Norman who made me feel guilty. I remember one time he cried when I said, "Fuck," and punted the basketball straight up in the air so that it landed on the roof of the McClellan's garage after he beat me one-on-one. It was then that I knew I was going to have to try to control my anger if I wanted Norman as a friend. So what I did was I developed this sort of coping mechanism, this little private system. Anytime I got angry around Norman I'd just make these really tight fists and squeeze. And I wouldn't say anything or move until I felt like it'd all just disappeared. Now keep in mind I was only ten at the time, so I'm sure Norman could tell I was angry anyway. But I think he was all right with it, as long as I didn't say "Fuck" or punt basketballs, or punch anything.

Most of the time this worked. I'd be able to calm myself down and not frighten Norman so much that he didn't want to play with me anymore. But something happened that night. Something happened as I sat there on the floor of the McClellan's upstairs living room. Something happened inside of me I think, that made it impossible for me not to show my anger, for me not to blow up the way my late father always seemed to blow up when something went wrong at work, or when my late mother made a terrible dinner, or when my brother John or I did something fucked up.

I remember squeezing my fists and thinking that I should just stop playing right then and there, that I should just grab all my stuff and put on my shoes and walk out the front door. I'd walk across the McClellan's front yard and jump down off the little brick wall into my late parent's front yard. And then I'd walk right past my late parent's house. I'd throw my stuff down in their yard because I didn't need it and just keep right on going. I'd walk until I couldn't walk anymore, till I collapsed in the woods somewhere, or disappeared into somebody's cornfield, or climbed a tree in somebody's apple orchard and passed out in the branches.

Of course, I didn't do any of those things.

Instead what I did was I picked the dice up off the score sheet and launched them at the window. They hit the glass so loud and so hard it made me think of that time Norman and I saw a cardinal fly smack into the windshield of Mrs. McClellan's Chevette. It made you jump if you didn't know it was coming.

If that had been the only thing that happened that night—if we hadn't been distracted, if our game hadn't been interrupted—I think all our lives would've been different. Maybe Norman never would've spoken to me again. Maybe the throwing of the dice would've been the last straw for him. Maybe the McClellans would've stopped letting me stay over all the time. Maybe I would've run away.

But, as luck would have it, right at the exact moment those dice were crashing against the upstairs living room window, Norman and I heard and felt something far more affecting: a very low sustained *boom* that I can only describe to you now as the sonic and tactile equivalent of the beating of a muffled bass drum. I remember the floor seemed to move, and I felt it in my stomach. I bet Norman did too, because we both stopped and looked at each other for a second (the dice now forgotten), and then turned and looked out the window at the sky.

Suddenly, there were footsteps on the stairs. Norman's older brother Andy appeared in the doorway of the living room. I seem to remember him wearing a faded black Rush *Roll the Bones* t-shirt, and I think it was the first time I had ever seen him wearing glasses. He looked at us and ran a hand through his hair, and half-whispered, half-spoke, "Did you hear that? D'you guys hear that?" I could hear Norman's parents moving in their bedroom down the hall. "It sounded like a bomb!" Andy shouted this time. "A fucking bomb!" he said, and stepped into the living room. Andy went and stood in front of the window and looked for something out on the horizon. "I don't see anything," he said. Norman and I got up and went and stood next to him. We too looked for something out on the horizon and we too didn't see anything.

It was simply as it always was: the cloudless early morning sky whose color we could never name, some faint neutral light off to the east; the autumn cornfield across the street, rolling slightly downhill to the south and the purple woods beyond; the tree line on the western edge of the cornfield, marking where the Cooper's property ended and the Whitney's property began.

I think I remember hearing the McClellan's rotary phone ring behind me in the kitchen just then, but I can't be sure. I was distracted by the little apple tree in the Cooper's front yard. I think it must've looked to me like someone who had no control of his body, planted waist down in the earth. The dark trunk was the torso, and the fruitless leafless limbs were the knotted bony arms that moved so fast they seemed still. I think I remember thinking the tree must've been possessed.

And then there was Mr. Cooper. He must've heard the *boom* too because he flung the screen door open and stood on his front step in his boxers and a bathrobe smoking an unfiltered Marlboro. His long black hair was not in a ponytail. His black ZZ Top beard swallowed what was left of his face. And the black and always-without-tires El Camino up on cinder blocks in the turnaround: it almost looked as if it too were part of the landscape, as if it too had somehow grown up out of the earth, a sick, diseased plant in need of care. (I would be shocked one evening the following summer when I walked out the McClellan's front door and saw the El Camino gone. Later, Andy would explain that Mr. Cooper had entered it in the Demolition Derby out at Spencer Speedway on 104 in Williamson and had placed first. I remember saying to no one in particular, "I wonder how the other drivers liked losing to a tree." Andy didn't answer.)

And of course, there was that flag—that dead-to-the-world Confederate flag Mr. Cooper always flew on the flag pole in his yard. We all must've seen it at the same time because Andy said, "There's no wind," right when I saw the flag hanging limp there on the pole. I seem to recall someone tapping me on the shoulder then too, but again I can't be sure. All I know is I was entranced by that flag, and the way it seemed to defy my ten-year-old logic that a *boom* that sounds like a "fucking bomb" could happen without a raging storm coming close on its heels.

But that's the way the weather was that morning, that's the way that I remember it: calm, surreal, like Gould's second recording of the Goldberg Variations.

That's what I remember.

That's what I remembered all at once the instant I saw the Plug-In Lamp & Appliance Timer, Model SB11C, by Intermatic, bought for $8.19 at Steven's Hardware at the back of my late father's desk.

That's what I remembered, and that was all.

At least until later.

Later, I would remember more.

In the car on the drive back home I would remember the rest of the story. My father's voice on the black rotary phone. And later the policeman, and the questions.

But these memories would not be of my own volition. No. It would be the tape. The TDK Cassette tape. That would be the trigger.

I remember I was driving back to Syracuse on the Thruway. I had just passed the Montezuma Wildlife Refuge and thought how depressing it was that we actually had to set aside and label pieces of land in order to keep them from disappearing. In order to keep them wild.

Then I turned away and looked out the driver side window: more dead trees sticking up out of the water. Dead hollow trees. A little creek.

After that I looked down at the passenger seat at the cardboard box filled with stuff from my late parent's house that I thought I might not want to throw away, so much stuff, in fact, that I hadn't been able to close the box, so much stuff, in fact, that some of the stuff fell out as I drove. Some stuff fell on the floor, and some fell next to the box. One of the things that fell next to the box was that tape, the unlabeled TDK Cassette tape—

———————————

I have to admit I'm feeling a little vulnerable right now. I'm not sure if I should be speaking of these things—for a number of reasons.

But this is only paper, right? I'm only writing it down. It can always be erased. I can always cut it up. I can always put it through a shredder or burn it if I want—

You can always fuck things up—

My late father didn't say much. Especially when he came home. And what he did say I don't remember very well. But that's one thing I do remember him saying a lot for real: *You can always fuck things up*—

So now I don't know what to do. I'd like to tell you what I heard that day in the car driving back to Syracuse. I'd love to tell you, believe me. But I'm not too sure I know what I heard. In fact I don't even know what I did with the tape. I don't have it anymore. So even if I wanted to, I couldn't go find it and listen to it again and transcribe the whole thing for you. And it's too bad, really, because with the equipment we've got at the Audio Lab I probably could've gotten rid of all the hissing and the noise I think I heard along with my late father's voice.

And it was his voice.

I know because I've got it in my head. It's not just one voice though. It's two or three voices coming from the same mouth. It's the voice I heard at home when all of us were there, my late father and my late mother and my brother John and I. That fucking non-specific voice. I can't give you any details or quote him at all. I just can't. All I can tell you is it was a very frightening voice, and that that's the way it always made me feel.

There's also the voice from the tape. I seem to recall it also being very non-specific. I can tell you this though: the voice on the tape was much calmer, and I seem to want to think it was talking about forgiveness. But it very well could've been talking about Elmer's Rubber Cement or Plug-In Lamp & Appliance Timers or something in the basement of Steven's Hardware. Or anything at all really. I remember it sounded like an interview, or part of an interview. As if the voice were answering questions. Except I don't recall hearing another voice on the tape (which, again, I definitely could've worked on, could've isolated and cranked up the volume on, with the equipment at the Audio Lab).

I also probably could've rolled up the window so I could hear better.

So what am I left with? What's concrete about it all? Nothing, really. The only thing close to concrete is that third voice I think I heard after the *boom* that interrupted me and Norman's Dice Baseball game. That voice I think I heard in the McClellan's kitchen on their black rotary phone. That *voice*—

I don't think I remember what it said, but I know the way it sounded. It was my father's voice, and it sounded scared. Scared and very far away. And even if I'm not sure he didn't say, "I'm sorry. You can always fuck things up," I think I'd like to think that that's what I was thinking with the phone up to my ear and my free-hand in a little fist at my side. I'd like to think that that's what I was thinking looking at the backs of the McClellans, standing side-by-side in their upstairs living room, silhouetted by that blank early morning sky, wondering about the *boom*—

Field notes

1.

Dad watches Mets games in the evening because he thinks he is supposed to watch Mets games in the evening. Mom watches Mets games with Dad because she thinks it is best for her to be subservient to Dad. Dad does not think Mom should be subservient to him necessarily, but he doesn't do or say anything to discourage her subservience. He lets her cook and clean and do the laundry, and he does not offer any help. He lets her get the groceries and take out the trash and go down to get the mail every day, and he does not offer any help. Dad is a retired US Postal Service worker, so to him his not-going-down-to-get-the-mail-every-day makes sense. The other things do not make sense, really—especially since it is true Dad does not think Mom should be subservient to him (necessarily). When he thinks of these things—the things that do not make any sense, really—he says to himself, "Some things don't make sense," and leaves it at that. Mom says this to herself too, when she thinks of these things that do not make any sense. (She says this with respect to other things about her marriage to Dad as well.) In this way, Dad and Mom have an understanding that works for them. They have erected a kind of system with which they can be satisfied. Or if not satisfied, perhaps comfortable.

2.

Dad is a well-liked Dad around the neighborhood. The neighborhood's name is Two Bridges. It is the neighborhood Dad grew up in and so it is the neighborhood he knows best. It is also the neighborhood of his old Postal route. Dad can mark time on many of the streets between the two Bridges by the names of the people who have lived there. It's a thing he does. Mom is a well-liked Mom around the neighborhood. It's the neighborhood she grew up in too, and so the neighborhood she knows best, too. Together, Dad and Mom know every block, and they can tell people every little thing that's happened there over the past sixty years or so. One of Dad's favorite memories involves Julius and Ethel Rosenberg. Dad lived in the apartment building next to theirs, and he remembers vividly the day he stood by the window and watched the FBI men lead the handcuffed Julius Rosenberg out of the apartment building, shame-faced and a Communist. Dad often thinks of this and wonders how many other people witnessed the FBI's arresting of Julius Rosenberg. "Not many," he thinks. Mom did not see the FBI's arresting of Julius Rosenberg. She lived in a different building on a different street and was probably playing pinochle with her cousins anyway. (She still plays pinochle with her cousins. Anyway.) One of Mom's favorite memories is the day she saw Montgomery Clift walking down East Broadway right after she saw *A Place in the Sun*. Mom was fifteen. Mom fell deeply in love with Clift that day and she is sure she has been deeply in love with him ever since. Clift's unfortunate car accident in Beverly Hills in 1956 and death ten years later were personal tragedies for Mom. She has never told Dad about her love for Montgomery Clift, but it is probably safe to say that Dad would not have cared: one's private life is one's own, after all. Dad and Mom are full of knowledge like this. They would never call this knowledge "knowledge," of course, but it is knowledge nonetheless. Or perhaps it is trivia. Either way.

3.

Dad and Mom live in the same apartment Dad and Mom have lived in for forty-eight years. Recently, the block in Two Bridges in which Dad and Mom's apartment is located has shown considerable improvement in terms of crime and demographic diversity. Dad often recalls the gritty, drug-addled 1980s when things seemed incredibly bad. Mom recalls the gritty, drug-addled 1980s too, but not as well or as often as Dad. This is perhaps because Dad was out in the neighborhood more than Mom. When Dad thinks of the 1980s now, he thinks of the so-called "crack epidemic" and what one might consider its odd juxtaposition with the greed and hand-over-fist-type moneymaking that was going on just a few blocks and one Bridge overpass to the south. Sometimes, when Dad is watching Mets games in the evening because he thinks he is supposed to watch Mets games in the evening, he notes how ironic it is that the team he is least proud of being a supporter of—the World Series-winning 1986 Mets—was also the team who had the most success. He has never been able to come to terms with the fact that the '86 Mets were a dominant "Fuck You"-type team who seemed to represent the City so well at the same time that their roster was loaded with cocaine and/or crack users and burgeoning alcoholics. He also notes how ironic it is that now that he has time to watch all the games he wants, he no longer wants to watch all the games. And yet: he does (continue to watch all the games). Mom does not note any irony about anything at all, ever. Or perhaps she does. Dad cannot be certain because Dad and Mom speak almost not at all.

4.

Nevertheless, there is one thing Dad feels he can be certain of: most women do not watch baseball on their own, without men. Dad has seen women watching baseball on their own without men on occasion, but he has concluded that most women doing this probably come from male-dominant families or communities in which the baseball team's games are considered a highly important social function. For them, Dad thinks, it is the social aspect that is the most important and/or interesting thing about baseball; whereas for men, the watching of the game of baseball is something that can be done either in private or in public, alone or with friends, sober or drunk. One can be elated or depressed. One can be nonplussed. One can be indifferent. It does not matter. It is only the watching of the game that matters. After Dad thinks this, he wonders if his watching Mets games with Mom is a private or a public affair. He never has an answer to this question and he's never asked Mom if she thinks their watching Mets games is a private or a public affair. Mom has never thought of watching Mets games in these terms. Or she has. Again, it is difficult to say with Mom.

5.

Nonetheless, over the years, Mom has internalized quite a lot about the game. She remembers player's names and faces very well, but has difficulty remembering numbers and positions. Mom always thinks of herself as a particularly fair Mom, and she has brought this to her watching and understanding of the game. Mom is a taker of copious notes. She leaves them stuck to walls and cabinets and mirrors all over the apartment. Most of them are reminders of jobs to do or groceries to get, but some of them are Bible verses or inspirational-type sayings. For example: "He that increaseth knowledge increaseth sorrow" (taped to the top of her dresser); or, "The patient in spirit is better than the proud in spirit" (on an orange Post-It note beside the light switch in the bedroom). None of them have anything to do with baseball. Since Dad retired from the US Postal Service, Mom has brought to her watching of the game of baseball with Dad her copious note-taking as well as her deep sense of fairness. She sits on the sofa and writes things down that occur to her as Dad keeps score. Mom especially likes to note little unfairnesses she observes about the rules of the game, unfairnesses such as these:

> "Why is the distance from home plate to the outfield wall different in every stadium? Every stadium in every city should be exactly the same size. It's only fair."

> "Why do pitchers bat in the National League but not in the American League? Either pitchers should bat in both leagues or pitchers should not

bat in both leagues. It should be one way or the other but not both."

"Why are you allowed to hit a ball in foul territory indefinitely after you have two strikes? Foul balls should either always be strikes or they should never count as balls or strikes at all."

"Why are you allowed to walk a player without giving him the opportunity to hit the ball? Pitchers should always have to try to throw the ball over home plate. There should be no intentional walks."

Mom keeps these in a little notebook. It's what keeps the game interesting to her and allows her to continue being subservient to Dad, which is what she thinks works best. Dad has never asked what Mom is doing when Mom is writing these things down. Mom has never asked what Dad is doing either, though, when he is writing his things down. It is just understood somehow. Their home is a quiet home.

6.

When Dad does not watch Mets games in the evening Dad can almost always be found reading. Dad did not go to college, but he grew up in a time when it was not standard for everyone to go to college. Dad got a good education in the New York City School System when it was possible for one to get a good education in the

New York City School System. A love of reading was instilled in Dad forever by his tenth grade English teacher. Like all readers, Dad has particular things he likes, but his working as a US Postal Service worker helped broaden and deepen his particular taste in reading. Among other things, Dad was a fast US Postal Service worker, and sometimes he would have the luxury of taking long lunches where he would read and eat and read and eat until the end of his shift. Dad has had periods where he read only science fiction novels, and periods where he read only presidential biographies, and periods where he read only about particular events or eras. For example, Dad has read every book there is on the life of Julius and Ethel Rosenberg. His interest in reading about Julius and Ethel Rosenberg led him to a novel called *The Public Burning* by Robert Coover. His reading of *The Public Burning* by Robert Coover led him to a book called *The Universal Baseball Association, Inc., J. Henry Waugh, Prop.*, also by Robert Coover. After Dad read this book, he thought he would try to read every book he could on baseball. Dad found out there are quite a lot of nonfiction books on baseball, but there are almost no books of fiction, most of which he thinks are not very interesting. Dad considers Ring Lardner's *You Know Me Al*, Philip Roth's *The Great American Novel*, Bernard Malamud's *The Natural*, Don DeLillo's *Underworld*, Robert Coover's *The Universal Baseball Association, Inc., J. Henry Waugh, Prop.* and Chad Harbach's *The Art of Fielding* perhaps the only interesting books about baseball in fiction. Something Dad has concluded from all this is that there are almost no good books of fiction about any sports and/or sports figures, practically. "Is this because people who are interested in sports don't read?" Dad wonders. "Do sports simply make a bad subject for

what fiction does best?" "Will none of us accept an athlete as a pro-
tagonist?" "Do John Updike's *Rabbit* books count?" Dad never has
an answer for any of these questions. Instead, he just waits for the
day when there will be a truly great American novel with baseball as
its subject. Or maybe he doesn't. Maybe he's sure there can't be one.

7.

In addition to Mom making notes about unfairnesses and incon-
sistencies in the rules of the game of baseball, Mom has also spent
a fair amount of time musing in her notebook on the loneliness she
thinks baseball players must feel. "Baseball is an odd sport," Mom
thinks. Each player is a part of a team, but one cannot observe in
baseball the obvious teamwork one sees in sports like basketball or
football or hockey. Mom notes that each player in baseball is almost
always doing things on his own on the field. There are whole games
Mom has seen where one player—for example, the right fielder—
never has the ball hit to him. When this happens, Mom watches
and thinks, "How lonely that must be. He just stands out there and
punches his glove and watches the ball get hit to other parts of the
field. He watches other players make plays and he just stands." Mom
particularly likes these players. She has little interest in, say, the
shortstop or third baseman, both of whom are always having the
ball hit to them. She has little interest in the first basemen or the
catcher as well, both of whom are always having the ball thrown to
them. She has little interest in pitchers, who always get to hold the
ball and who dictate the pace of the game by deciding how long
they will take between pitches. Mom wonders what all the play-

ers are thinking, it is true, but she wonders most about the right fielder—"what do right fielders think about when they're out there and nothing is happening?" This question is especially vexing to Mom because she has seen post-game interviews with players and they almost always give the same answers about just playing each game "one game at a time" and about how they are just "lucky to be members of the team" and such, and as a result Mom has come to believe that all baseball players are probably very unintelligent, which makes her wonder if maybe right fielders just stand out there and punch their glove thinking about nothing but standing out there and punching their glove. Mom of course has never asked Dad what he thinks baseball players are thinking about when they are out there on the field. She of course hasn't asked about that.

8.

Something that is true: Dad misses his job as a US Postal Service worker. He still has his uniform and sometimes, when Mom has taken a taxi to the grocery store or gone out to run some other errand, he will go into their bedroom and get the uniform out and place it on Mom's bed and sit on his bed and look at his uniform on her bed. Sometimes he will put it on and look at himself in the mirror and consider the lines in his face. Sometimes he just looks at the uniform on the bed and thinks about things that have happened or things he once saw out on his route: Mrs. Markowitz and her cat on a leash on their way to Seward Park; the difficulty of the door at 5 Market Street; a man frozen to death in the alley behind St. Joseph's; long lunches eating and reading by himself at the deli on East Broadway; the smothered sound of dogs barking in distant apartments in various buildings. Et cetera. Dad misses his job as a US Postal Service worker. Et cetera.

9.

One time Mom comes home from the grocery store and finds Dad sitting on his bed looking at his US Postal Service worker uniform. Dad's hearing is almost gone, so he does not hear Mom walk down the hall to the doorway to their bedroom. Mom watches Dad and wonders how lonely he is. She has the urge to walk in and console him, but she does not want to offend him or embarrass him or do anything that would make him feel uncomfortable. Mom looks at her watch. It is 3:45 in the afternoon. She turns and walks down the hall to the living room. She sits on the couch and turns on the TV. A Mets game is on. Mom gets out her notebook and finds a fresh scorecard for Dad and puts it on the coffee table in front of the sofa. Mom has DVR'd the game because she knows Dad likes to have a complete scorecard and he would be upset if he missed anything. Some minutes later Dad comes down the hall to the living room too. He sits down and starts keeping score without saying a word to Mom. He is thinking about his old Postal route. He is thinking about how there are no good books of fiction on baseball. He is thinking about the '86 Mets. He is thinking about the time he saw a man frozen to death behind the gate in the alley behind St. Joseph's on Catherine Street. He is thinking about Julius and Ethel Rosenberg. He is not thinking about Montgomery Clift. He is not thinking about *A Place in the Sun*. He is not thinking about the various unfairnesses of the rules of the game of baseball. He is not thinking about how lonely baseball players must be in their heads out there on the field. He is not thinking about Mom. He is not he is not he is not.

WALT'S WALTZ

I am pacing in the hallway outside the press room outside the club-house next to the very red door that leads into the manager's office. I have one of those waxy paper cups in my off-hand and it feels sort of half-wet ever since I finished the mysterious Gatorade-Water-Vita-min concoction our team's trainer gave me to drink. I can hear the trainer's footsteps on the hallway's cement floor as he approaches the end of the hallway and is, I know, about to turn back toward the sloped ramp that leads back out onto the hallway that leads to the other sloped ramp that leads you out onto the field. The manager and our pitching coach, Dave, and probably also the first- and third base-coaches are in the manager's office going over the details of my performance. I am outside waiting, pacing. Félix, our injured second baseman, is sitting on the floor and leaning up against the white-and red-striped wall in the hallway and is squeezing what appears to be a racquetball every half second or so and saying *corazón de pollo* over and over as he squeezes. I can't tell if he is talking about me or not. Every five or so minutes Félix stops squeezing the racquetball and throws it at one particular brick across the hallway's expanse, trying always to hit the same brick, which he does, easily and with-out fail, remarking, every time the ball *pock*s against the center of the brick, in loud and Dominican-inflected English, *cha-ching!*, as if he's ringing up the money he stands to make this year without even having to step on the field for a single regular season game. I can feel the heat in the balls of my feet and their soreness inside my cleats. My shoulder—the pitching one—feels as if it's been placed at some point in the not-too-distant past inside a very large and perpetually tightening vise grip. This image makes me think of my father, who is, no doubt at this very moment sweeping the sidewalk in front of the steps of his apartment building a couple thousand miles to the east. I have a kind of vague notion that an invisible but very much real box or cage or maybe even some kind of strange force-field-like thing exists around the parameters of my actual physical self. This is not something I or anyone else with the club can ever see, but it's something that has seemed to be present for the better part of a year now for me—a year in which I've seen my WHIP jump up about sixty-five percent and my ERA go up about six runs to 9.25. These are numbers Dave gives me as we sit out in the bullpen four of five days a week and chew seeds and spit shells and make remarks about the opposing team's outfielders just loud enough for them to hear. I don't know these numbers off the top of my head when I'm on the field. I can't; it would kill me. I can sense them, yes; I can tell there is something very, very wrong going on here. I have balked at least once in every start since June. I am pacing. I am pacing. The sound of the spikes of my cleats against the cement reminds me of the sound Veronica's nails make when she drums them on the Formica countertop in my kitchen. I hear them—the spikes—and then I hear them again, and then I hear the first one overtop of the second, and then the second overtop of the first overtop of the second, and then the first overtop of the second overtop of the first overtop of the second, and I start to feel as if I'm on a kind of acid trip, as if this scene is one I've either been in before or one I am not, in reality, a physical part of. It's like I am there and not-there. Like when I'm on the mound and I'm in the Zone. When Mike's mitt behind the plate is the size of a watermelon and I can pick out corners and make the ball break or drop or kick back in on itself in ways the hitter can't do anything about. Except not like that. Not like that at all. It hasn't been like that for months, and even then only in warm-ups, or only on off-days, or only when I'm not on the mound. Now it's like this, like this all the time, like this here in the hallway. Félix a kind of sidekick to me; "Félix, come along to keep [me] out of [my] head." Félix and his racquetball and his *corazón de pollo* and the *pock* of the ball and its subsequent echo reverberating through the hallway's walls and the cooly air-conditioned air here deep inside our stadium's trenches, the kind of air that feels sort of halfway real and halfway manufactured, the air that fills up our lungs in the clubhouse, all of us sitting serenely on our stools in front of our lockers, our jerseys hanging like nothing else will hang on a hanger, stiff and heavy and thick, our names stitched in red in large block letters with black shadow trim—ECCLES behind ECCLES behind ECCLES behind ECCLES—home, away, Sunday, and practice, the little cardinals sitting placid and bemused on either end of the bat on the front of the jerseys, balancing it carefully, one on either end, balancing, weighting things perfectly, not even having to think about what it is they're doing but just doing it, just brainstem and no-brain, just landing there, alighting, just birds being birds being birds being birds…I am pacing. I am pacing and I'm certain I know

what's being said behind the manager's door. Félix is certain, too.
He is saying, "I dunno, man. Mex says this is it. I know you don't
wanna hear that, but that's what Mex says." Mex is an L. A.-born
long reliever who's been with the club for twelve years. Mex played
Double-A with the manager and is the same age. Mex is a vet. Mex
knows what Mex knows. Mex is not Mexican but he grew up with
Mexicans and was adopted as a kid by Mexican parents. So Mex
is pretty much Mexican. Mex knows what Mex knows what Mex
knows. I am pacing. I am pacing and I'm waiting and I'm trying to
make at least a kind of half-sense of what it is that's happened to
my arm or happened to my brain or happened to my arm's brain.
My off-arm is fine. I sit down next to Félix now and hear myself tell
him, "My off-arm, it's fine." Félix laughs and throws the ball across
the hallway and hits the same brick he's been hitting with a *pock*
and then says, "I don't think it's your off-arm you need to be worried
about, man," as he catches the ball without even having to move.
I am pissed royally at Félix for being here and for being Félix, and
I am pissed royally at myself for being here and being myself. The
lighting in this hallway adds to the sense I have of being somehow
here and not-here. I think I can hear it working (the lighting, that is).
It is fluorescent and white and it sounds like a giant bug zapper with
the volume turned down. It's humming like an industrial fan or a
bee-swarm somewhere nearby you can't ever seem to locate. The
door to the manager's office is very, very red now. I haven't hit Mike's
mitt in official league play in something like four starts. The fans
are wearing helmets to the stadium when it's my day to pitch. The
door seems to be almost kind of glowing red now as I sit here. I can
feel the manager approaching. I can feel him stepping toward me

and Félix. Félix is saying *su corazón de pollo, su corazón de pollo.* I cannot see the manager approaching from behind the thrumming-red door but it is somehow clear he is, he is. The lights overhead like a heartbeat. My heart like the thump of a bird on a windshield on I-70. This is not good. No, this is not good at all.

Quartet (3)

In the summer of 2008, I was living with a woman from Québec named Marie and a young man from Somerset, England named Samuel in an apartment that overlooked the Nile and that was the closest thing to quiet one could get in a city like Cairo. Silence—or at least the capacity for silence—was important because all of us were in Egypt for the sole purpose of improving our Arabic, which was itself important because all of us were Middle East studies majors at large east coast US universities. It's not important here why I was studying this. What is important is that one day, sitting at the table in the corner of the living room with Marie, I came across a quotation in a French-language paper that, as far as I could tell, ought to have been published in something like *The Onion*, because I could not for the life of me begin to believe it was true. What it was was an interview with a former high-ranking public official, who was himself a personal assistant and sort of lackey to another, higher-ranking public official—an official who some say, perhaps, was the most powerful man in the world at one time. A string-puller, a silent assassin, a man who wielded power and shaped minds without ever having to seem as if he were doing so—a sort of Wizard of Oz of US government, an Iago in a blue suit and a red tie with an American flag pin on his lapel. The quote was sort of tossed off, and in fact I recall that it had nothing to do with the question that had been asked of the high-ranking official. I cannot recall the context of the question or the answer now, and it's been a long time since I've seen the notebook in which I copied down what's about to follow. But, nevertheless, the gist of it was that the high-ranking official's boss—a man who'd been in government since the 1960s—secretly had always wished to be a mystery writer. He'd been a fan of Paul Auster and Patricia Highsmith, and especially admired the works of that now little-read Englishman, G. K. Chesterton. I found this highly amusing: a man whom I'd considered perhaps the closest thing to evil incarnate inside the US government sitting down to read *The New York Trilogy* or *The Talented Mr. Ripley* or *The Man Who Was Thursday* in the offices of the White House? A man whose smile perhaps couldn't even accurately be described as anything but a smirk or half-smirk because it was only on one side of his face and was only always accompanied by a raised eyebrow and his unblinking crystal blue eyes—this man? He read novels and wanted to write them? It only got worse as I read on and the high-ranking official's loquaciousness got the best of him as he revealed that not only did his boss read and want to write mystery novels, he in fact had the great ambition of wanting to write his generation's *Moby-Dick*, because he felt that in some way he, the higher-ranking official, could accurately be described as a combination of Ishmael, Ahab, and the Whale, and that his distinguished or infamous career— depending on which side you were on—in US politics could actually be read into the text of Melville's great work.

Well, this I just couldn't believe, and so I set the paper down and told Marie I was going out to smoke some shisha and that I'd be back in an hour or so. An hour or so passed the way an hour or so passes in a hookah bar. And, in fact, the remainder of the summer passed the very same way. I studied my Arabic, visited the ancient pyramids, argued in broken Arabic and furious English with Cairo's taxi drivers, and returned to D. C. in August having completely forgotten everything I'd read about the high-ranking official's boss.

Two-and-a-half months later, I was in the middle of an extended session in the library when I decided I'd take a break and read the paper. When I opened it up I read that the high-ranking official's boss had passed away the previous evening. He'd had a weak heart, and had had several heart attacks throughout his later years. But this latest one had been too much, and he'd died of heart failure at his home with his family. Immediately, I recalled the interview I'd read in the French-language paper, particularly its absurdity, and I decided right then and there I'd write a letter to the high-ranking official telling him I was a graduate student at Georgetown in the Middle East studies program, but that I'd recently had a change of heart and wanted, now, to examine US involvement in that region, and the recent death of his now late-boss was of particular interest to me given his particular interest in the region during his tenure in the White House. At the end of the letter I mentioned I'd read an interview he'd given to the French-language paper, and was interested in his boss' interest in literature, namely his desire to write his generation's *Moby-Dick*, and that if he knew of or had access to any literary material his boss had written, I'd greatly appreciate being able to have a look at it—in facsimile form, of course—or some part or parts of it, as it would be indescribably helpful in gaining an understanding of the man. I signed it, dated it, mailed it through official Georgetown University mail and quietly went back about my business as a Middle East studies major.

Several weeks passed. I was, again, nose-deep in my studies and had more or less forgotten the letter I'd sent to the high-ranking official, despite the media's constant coverage of the higher-ranking official's funeral and burial, and the subsequent appearance of various family members and former co-workers on news shows on almost every channel. I'd sent the letter as a lark, and didn't even expect to receive a complimentary "thank you for your interest"-type reply.

Imagine my surprise, then, when I checked my mail slot near the end of the semester and found an envelope with the high-ranking official's return address on it. I opened it immediately and read that the high-ranking official was delighted I'd read his interview with the French-language paper and that the higher-ranking official's family would themselves be delighted to have some young scholar help preserve their father's legacy the way it ought to be preserved: as that of a great political man who was, ultimately, a misunderstood and failed artist, and that enclosed in the envelope at the family's behest were some fragments of a text the higher-ranking official had been working on from time to time, right up until the day he died. The high-ranking official thanked me again for my interest, and said that as co-executor of his former boss' estate—the other co-executor was the higher-ranking official's daughter—he looked forward to meeting me and my thesis advisor sometime soon. The letter ended there, and I promptly shuffled it to the back of the pile

of papers and started in on what was purportedly one of the fragments the higher-ranking official had been working on before he
died. What I read that day still shocks me and the shock can only
be fully communicated through at least a partial reading of the text
itself. Here is what I read that day:

"What the great man was to others, has been hinted; what, at
times, he was to me, as yet remains unsaid.

"Aside from those more obvious considerations touching the
great man, which could not but occasionally awaken in any man's
soul some alarm, there was another thought, or rather vague, nameless horror concerning him, which at times by its intensity completely overpowered all the rest; and yet so mystical and well nigh
ineffable was it, that I almost despair of putting it in a comprehen-
sible form. It was the whiteness of the man that above all things
appalled me.

"Though in many natural objects, whiteness refiningly enhances
beauty, as if imparting some special virtue of its own, as in marbles,
japonicas, and pearls; and though various nations have in some
way recognised [sic] a certain royal pre-eminence in this hue; even
the barbaric, grand old kings of Pegu placing the title 'Lord of the
White Elephants' above all their other magniloquent ascriptions
of dominion; and the modern kings of Siam unfurling the same
snow-white quadruped in the royal standard; and the Hanoverian
flag bearing the one figure of a snow-white charger; and the great
Austrian Empire, Cæsarian heir to overlording Rome, having for
the imperial color the same imperial hue; and though this pre-eminence in it applies to the human race itself, giving the white man
ideal mastership over every dusky tribe; and though, besides all this,

whiteness has been even made significant of gladness, for among the Romans a white stone marked a joyful day; and though in other mortal sympathies and symbolizings, this same hue is made the emblem of many touching, noble things—the innocence of brides, the benignity of age; though among the Red Men of America the giving of the white belt of wampum was the deepest pledge of honor; though in many climes, whiteness typifies the majesty of Justice [sic] in the ermine of the Judge [sic], and contributes to the daily state of kings and queens drawn by milk-white steeds; though even in the higher mysteries of the most august religions it has been made the symbol of the divine spotlessness and power; by the Persian fire worshippers the white forked flame being held the holiest on the altar; and in the Greek mythologies, Great Jove himself being made incarnate in a snow-white bull; and though to the noble Iroquois, the mid-winter festival of their theology, that spotless, faithful creature being held the purest envoy they could send to the Great Spirit with the annual tidings of their own fidelity; and though directly from the Latin word for white, all Christian priests derive the name of one part of their sacred vesture, the alb or tunic, worn beneath the cassock; and though among the holy pomps of the Romish faith, white is specially employed in the celebration of the Passion of our Lord; though in the Vision of St. John, white robes are given the redeemed, and the four-and-twenty elders stand clothed in white before the great white throne, and the Holy One that sitteth there white like wool; yet for all these accumulated associations, with whatever is sweet, and honorable, and sublime, there yet lurks an elusive something in the innermost idea of this hue, which strikes more of panic to the soul than that redness which affrights blood."

The text goes on like this for several pages. My great disappointment of course was that the higher-ranking official hadn't really
written anything. What he'd done in this fragment was change six
words of the original text of chapter 42—the chapter entitled "The
Whiteness of the Whale"—of Melville's *Moby-Dick*, and that is all.

I'm still not sure what the disappointment I felt that day can be
attributed to. At first I thought it had to do with the fact that the
higher-ranking official turned out not to be working on anything
other than copying or transcribing. But this thought disturbed me,
because it seemed to indicate I had wanted the higher-ranking official to be writing a work of literary genius, and if this was what
I had in fact wanted it of course meant that I'd wanted, in some
way, a man I considered evil and strange and devilish in the political sphere to be brilliant and strange and devilish in the literary
sphere—and what on earth could possibly be behind an idea like
that?

Later, I considered the idea that I was disappointed I hadn't found
some sort of confession or honest assessment the man gave of himself in his writing he couldn't ever seem to give in public. This,
to me, meant I'd hoped to find the "true man" in his writing, the
man I didn't know. When I did not find this—when all I found was
appropriation—I felt validated in my belief that he was, in fact, evil
and strange and devilish. This seemed infinitely worse though, if
for no other reason than that what it meant was that we'd elected
an evil, strange, and devilish man not once but twice to one of the
most powerful offices in the world. At the time I couldn't think of
anything more despairing.

Several months later, I thought of something else, and this is where I tend to stand today. The higher-ranking official's replacement of "white whale" for "great man" in this particular section of *Moby-Dick* seems telling. Because if he sees himself as the white whale as seen through Ishmael's eyes, he essentially sees himself as "appalling" and as someone who "strikes more panic to the soul than that redness which affrights blood," which of course means he perhaps did see himself the way I saw him then—at least in some small part of himself.

I never contacted the high-ranking official again after that first correspondence. In fact, I sent the envelope and its contents back to its return address. The only thing I have today is a photocopy of the altered Melville text in what I assume to be the handwriting of the former higher-ranking official. I have promised the family I will not pursue this issue any further.

Deposition

"This guy I met at a bar the other night told me an unbelievable story. Actually, I didn't really meet him and he wasn't really talking to me, either. He was telling the bartender this story about a teacher he'd had in grade school. From the way he was talking about it though, you could tell he didn't really care if anyone overheard him. It was almost like he was proud of it in a way.

"He was talking about this teacher he'd had, and this really kind of gross incident that occurred over at the teacher's house one night—this highly inappropriate situation that clearly shouldn't even have been allowed to happen in the first place and that definitely would've gotten the teacher fired if there'd been any proof.

"There wasn't any proof though, this guy said, because it was just him and the teacher at the teacher's house, and the teacher was a really popular teacher—you know, the kind of teacher all the kids want to have and all the parents lobby for their kids to have the summer before their kids go into the grade the teacher teaches in. Just a really great grade school teacher. So great, the guy said, that even his own parents didn't believe him when he told them what happened. That's how popular the teacher was.

"I didn't get this all right away, by the way. The guy had a tendency to repeat himself, and when I first came in I wasn't even really listening just yet. Sure, I was aware there was this guy around the corner of the bar telling a story to the bartender, yeah. But that's just about all I was aware of at first.

"One of the first things I was aware of when I started paying attention was the bartender. I could tell right away he wasn't the kind of bartender who just casually listens. I mean he was really listening. You know, like really into it. Not *into it* into it like he got off on it, though maybe he did, I don't know, but into it like he thought the story was just ridiculously interesting and good. What's that phrase? 'Beyond the pale'? Beyond the pale. Like this story was just beyond the pale. Sure, he was doing his job, tending bar and getting everyone's drinks and everything, but this kind of thing was second nature to him: he could probably get people's drinks in his sleep. I've been to a lot of bars and gotten a lot of drinks from a lot of bartenders, so believe me when I say I can tell if they're really listening to you versus when they're just kind of nodding along, placating. I pay attention to these things—especially if it's a bar I've never been in, which at the time this bar was. At the time, I was working construction on this site over on Eleventh Avenue. It was July and hot as hell, and every day after work I got in this habit of stopping off at a different bar on my way over to the East Side to get the train back uptown. Just for the hell of it. Just because might as well check out the bars while I'm here, right? This was maybe the third different bar I'd been in that week. It was dark inside and almost cold. There wasn't any music on and everybody looked like they'd been there forever. A real neighborhood bar. But not the kind of place where people stare at you when you walk in if they've never seen you before. It was more the kind of place where if you don't bother anyone nobody cares if you're there or not.

"Anyway, when I came in this guy was right in the middle of the story. Or he'd already started it, anyway. The bartender came over and took my order but he didn't even really look at me. Like I said, he was just totally wrapped up in what this guy was saying. So obviously I start to wonder what's so interesting about this guy, what's so great about what he's talking about. And so then I start listening in too as the bartender's getting my drink, and when I start to realize what he's talking about, it's like 'Holy fucking shit!' I start watching him then because now I'm interested, and just as soon as I do I can tell he's pretty drunk. Not *drunk* drunk, but drunk. Feeling good, let's say. And he was talking so much and so fast he didn't even really have any time to take a sip of his drink. The story was all he was doing. This was the guy's reason to be just then: to tell this story in this bar among these particular people at this particular time. He had these glasses that kept sliding down his nose every time he got worked up about a particular part of the story, these horn-rimmed things he kept pushing back up his nose with his middle finger. He would actually make the gesture of giving you the finger when he did this. And every once in a while he'd pound the bar with his fist like he was trying to make his point more forceful or something.

"After he did this a couple of times I started to feel really weird about him—even weirder than I felt about everything he was talking about. I started to think 'This guy's not telling the truth at all.' I started to think he was just sitting there around the corner of the bar lying his fucking face off. I don't know why. It just felt that way. It just felt…false. Like he was telling the story a certain way because he'd seen it told that way before. Like acting, right? Like 'Oh I know this scene: it's just like that scene in X,' you know? Like it was right out of a movie or something. And it wasn't because the story was *so* unbelievable, it wasn't because the story was *so* outrageous or anything like that. I mean yeah it was unbelievable and outrageous to an extent, but still. I mean Catholic Church, right? It was more just his mannerisms and everything. This middle finger business and the horn-rimmed glasses and the pounding of the bar. Like 'Hey, everybody look at me!' It really started to piss me off after a while. Like 'Who the hell does this guy think he is telling this story in a bar? Who the hell does he think he is telling something like that out loud in public?'

"Anyway, so now you can imagine I start getting pretty worked up too. I'm just like this other guy, except I'm getting worked up for real. Or at least it feels that way. I'm actually sitting there getting angry at *him*, at this guy I don't even know in a bar I've never been in, in a neighborhood where I'm a stranger because of a story where *he's* the victim. I'm even getting ready to say something. You know, sitting there getting ready to call his lying ass out, to call his bluff—just to see how he reacts. To see if he's ready to throw down or if he's just full of shit or whatever.

"But then I get to thinking, 'You know what? I've seen this scene, too.' It's the scene where the stranger walks into a bar and challenges the local, the scene where the film's hero—the Outsider—comes to town and challenges the villain to a duel. And then I start thinking about guns and Westerns and mesas and John Wayne and Clint Eastwood and shacking up with the starlet and things like that. And this gets me real down, it gets me *real* down. I get so down in fact I decide I probably shouldn't say anything at all. Because who the fuck am I, right? Who the fuck am I to challenge this guy I don't even know? I should probably just keep to myself. I should probably just finish my beer and throw down my money and head home.

"And this is what I do.

"More or less."

Quartet (4)

It's 2015. The setting is Astoria, Queens. A young man in a beard and a winter hat sits at his desk finishing a story he's certain is unlike anything he's ever seen. The young man has an incredible amount of anxiety about how the story will be read. Perhaps his main concerns are that it's a) boring, b) pretentious, c) a total mess, d) unfun, or e) some combination of any and all of a)-d).

As is often the case in stories like this—stories in which someone is uncertain about something they've written—the young man knows very little beyond the fact that he felt, at some point, there was a story to be told there. He'd seen through-lines and parallels and had felt certain there was something to be said in a way that no one else had said it, and that this was good because for him this should always be the goal of any writer: to say new things, or at least to find new ways of saying old things. And of course, when he got down to thinking about it all, that's sort of what was going on in the story he was trying to tell. He'd drawn confidently upon the idea that even someone like, say, Shakespeare was an appropriator of stories, and that the interpretation of something like, say, *The Wizard of Oz* seemed almost always to be botched perhaps because of the fact that it had been retold so many times and that the version almost everyone got to know was the version Hollywood had told, and that attempts at projecting and transposing figures like former US vice president Dick Cheney onto something like *Moby-Dick*—itself a kind of appropriated story or amalgamation of "true" sea stories of the day—seemed like a good idea, because one of the evilest-seeming things about someone like Dick Cheney to the young man was his whiteness, his pure Republican corporate ivory tower whiteness, and this seemed to fit well with the famous "The Whiteness of the Whale" chapter, the purported piece of nonfiction inside the fiction, an essayish moment in what's considered by many to be the greatest work of US fiction ever produced.

Somewhere along the line though, things went off the rails for the young man. He'd planned to draw some sort of parallel between the unwarranted evil of an Iago in *Othello*—also known as the ensign in Cinthio's original 1565 Italian short story "Un Capitano Moro"—the fraudulent Wizard in L. Frank Baum's *The Wonderful Wizard of Oz*, and the seemingly unwarranted evil of a behind-the-scenes string-puller like former US vice president Dick Cheney. There was also going to be lots of little asides and tangents on the nature of storytelling, and because of this it seemed like a good idea to the young man to tell the three stories from the point of view of the storyteller himself, to tell the story of how the story was written and/or told, while of course also being sure to make reference to the other sections of this story in the telling of how the telling of the other stories got told. It all got jumbled up, though. The *Wizard of Oz* section was less interesting than the *Othello* section: it ended far too abruptly, and really just basically sat there, deader than dead on the page. The *Othello* section itself was too long. It had a kind of propulsive movement, yes, but that's about it. The *Moby-Dick*/Cheney section seemed as if it might be better off as a thing on its own—a standalone story that could be expanded and enriched rather than the third section of a four-part story that isn't even a story, really. In other words: it started to seem to the young man that what he was doing with this stuff—imposing a kind of metafiction—that is to say, fiction about the making of fiction[16]— perhaps really couldn't be used sincerely as a way to get at genuine truths about what it's like to live in a world that's full of irony and reference and coy knowingness and people who seem to be familiar with absolutely everything all the fucking time. This was a great disappointment to the young man, because he'd felt certain that if he tried hard enough metafiction could be used this way. Instead, what it seemed to do in his story—his story being the story of the telling of these stories—above all else was annoy. It was presumptuous about certain things he hadn't ever thought he'd find himself being presumptuous about—namely, the fact that people probably don't need to be reminded that what they're reading is fiction and perhaps sometimes all anybody wants is to be entertained.[17]

And so, despite the fact that the young man still considered it basically insane and impossible for him to write anything that didn't somehow refer to itself—since a) this was how it felt to him to be a human being in 2015, and b) the very possibility of self-referentiality was, to him, one of the major things that made humans human and

---

16. I.e., "[Fiction] in which the forms of fiction serve as the material upon which further forms can be imposed" (William H. Gass, "Philosophy and the Form of Fiction," *Fiction and the Figures of Life*, 25).

17. Because: the effect on the reader of much of his story seemed to him to have the same effect as having a conversation with a stranger who keeps reminding you, *in conversation* and without regard for what the conversation's actually about, that one day you're going to die.

not some other species—the young man struck a deal with himself: he said he'd work much harder next time to try to come up with ways he could use metafiction and its inherent irony as a means to a useful end, an end that was much more along the lines of traditional storytelling with characters—though of course, he protested to himself, he'd always had those (even in the most meta- of all his metafictions)—and scenes—though of course, he protested to himself again, he'd always had those as well—and whatever else one needs to be sure one includes in works of prose fiction. And furthermore, the young man wanted to be sure he'd understood himself that no matter what, his goal had not been to seem smart or clever, because he hadn't wanted to "look like a self-consciously inbent shmuck, or like just another manipulative pseudopomo bullshit artist who's trying to salvage a fiasco by dropping back to a meta-dimension and commenting on the fiasco itself," because that of course would look pathetic and certainly wouldn't allow readers the opportunity "to pretend they believe the literary artist who wrote what they're reading" did so in order to try to help them "escape the insoluble flux of themselves [by] enter[ing] a world of prearranged meaning" that makes it seem like yes there *are* in fact people in the world who "deep inside experience things the same way you do,"[18] which to the best of the young man's knowledge was basically what everyone was searching for all the time in everything they did: a way to feel as if they're part of something larger, be it religious, political, familial, fraternal, sororital, national, continental, global, or universal. Or any other hermeneutical part-whole schema one could come up with.

---

18. David Foster Wallace, "Octet," *Brief Interviews with Hideous Men*, 159–60.

The point, the young man felt, was that he wasn't certain he'd been doing the work of fiction in his fiction, and the possibility that he might not have been frightened him to the point of paralysis. Because then what to do now? Where to go from here? Everything seemed a total mess, and what it all came down to, he thought, was whether this was okay, whether the mess was the point, whether the mess felt to him more like reality than some sort of representation of reality, whether it was worth it, whether fiction ought to feel more real, whether "more real" even makes any sense, whether anybody else felt at all the same way, and that if they did what did that mean? And if they didn't what did *that* mean? Whether the honesty with which he felt he was writing was really just another layer of faux-honesty, a fiction, and that deep-down what was really going on was that he was representing the representation of honesty by writing about writing when clearly nobody but perhaps a small percentage of other writers gives a fuck about writing about writing, and that really many, many, many authors who have come before him have already done this kind of thing with greater success,[19] and that really what one ought to do is just go ahead and suspend one's disbelief and enjoy the experience of reading something good and true and alive and real, whatever that might be.

It was with this in mind that the young man stopped thinking and went to bed. He was aware he hadn't made any real decision just

19. See, for example, the story cited in FN 18, just above. Also, any of the following: Cervantes' *Don Quijote*; Sterne's *Tristram Shandy*; Fielding's *Tom Jones*; Coleridge's "Kubla Khan; Or, A Vision in a Dream. A Fragment"; Melville's *Moby-Dick* and *The Confidence-Man*; Joyce's *Ulysses* and *Finnegans Wake*; much of Virginia Woolf; most of Samuel Beckett; Flann O'Brien's *At Swim-Two-Birds*; Jorge Luis Borges; Nathalie Sarraute's *Tropismes* and *Le Planétarium*; Robbe-Grillet's *La Jalousie*; Nabokov's *Pale Fire*; Italo Calvino; John Barth; Donald Barthelme; Robert Coover; David Markson; Michael Martone; Coetzee's *Elizabeth Costello*; Enrique Vila-Matas's *Bartleby & Co.*; et al., et al., et al.

yet, but he was also aware that he hoped he'd wake up the next day with something better to tell, and perhaps a better way to tell it. He of course didn't count on this, though.[20]

---

20. "Αὔριον ἄδιον ἄσω*," he thought.
*"I shall sing a sweeter song tomorrow," Theocritus, *Idyls*, 1.145.

Zeno's parachute

The man, who is me, wants to understand time. He remembers, among many other things, these in particular: summer afternoons in the basement of his parent's house, television, VCRs, bird-drawing, oscillating roundhead fans, the appearance of a shed in the northeast corner of the backyard that housed axes and sawhorses and shingles and mowers and snowblowers and other things he was not to touch.

He remembers feeling something he called *boredom*. *Boredom* was the result of having no one around to play with or talk to. When he thinks of *boredom* now it seems something like the flu: it was felt all over the body and was dreadful in a way he was not prepared to deal with and so didn't.

Later, he is out in the garage with his father. He is holding a piece of a wood his father cannot hold and work on at the same time. His father's boring holes in the wood for something I cannot recall but that surely must still be somewhere in my parent's house doing something worthwhile, twenty years later. This was boring, too. I think generally of times I had to help my father when I could hear other children in the neighborhood doing other things that sounded fun.

Another time, later, there is afternoon golf or afternoon bowling on the television. It seems to take forever for the golfers to decide what to do and when they finally do decide what to do that takes forever, too. They hand their club to the caddy and the two of them walk to where the ball was hit and take forever to decide what to do again, forever. Clearly, the afternoon golf and afternoon bowling could not have been on at the same time. And yet, they are somehow part of the same generalized memory. I watch as he watches the bowling ball's rapid circular movement inside the circular movement of the ball in an arc across the lacquered lane and wonder how anyone could find something like bowling a worthwhile way to spend one's time.

A long time ago, when the man was just a boy, his brother's car was stalled in the driveway behind his mother's car. The boy's brother and the boy's father had to push the brother's car out of the driveway so the boy's mother could drive her car to the store. The boy's father told the boy to sit in the driver seat and steer the car while he and the boy's brother pushed. The boy was very excited. He opened the driver side door and sat on the edge of the seat and put his very small hands on the very large wheel. The brother and the father pushed the car backward out of the driveway and into the road. The road has a bend in it. The boy was turning the wheel to the right so they could push the car back into the driveway down next to the mother's car so she could back out. But then the boy heard the brother shout. He stopped turning the wheel. The father said something too, perhaps, and the boy looked and saw the brother running away from the car into the neighbor's yard across the street. The boy was scared then, but wasn't sure why. One or two seconds later, he

understood: another car had come around the bend and was moving very fast and looked as if it wasn't going to stop. I remember
this very clearly.

Later, I was trying to write something and felt like a fraud. Later,
I was walking in a neighborhood that felt unsafe. Some other time
someone watched me on the train for a long time and then got off
two stops before me. Once, the boy was hit with a baseball when he
was eight and he remembers seeing the ball's rotation and its little
red seams just before it struck him and cut his eyebrow and part of
his right eyelid. A high fever produced hallucinations before the boy
had ever eaten mushrooms or dissolved confetti squares of acid on
his tongue. Munch's *The Scream*. The Man in the Gray Flannel Suit
who stepped out of the mirror at the end of the upstairs hallway and
walked toward him as he watched TV with his mother. A Christmas
decoration of a woman in a blue velvet robe with a flat, featureless,
gold-foil face. Some other things, and then some other things, too.
And waste, waste, waste.

Photograph and illustration credits

p. 60—"Overhead view of present-day New York…" by Thomas Cotsonas

p. 62—"Astoria Pool, Astoria, Queens…" by Thomas Cotsonas

p. 64—"New York City Department of Parks and Recreation logo…" by Thomas Cotsonas

p. 67—"Moses destroying the ten commandments and golden calf" by Graffisimo, courtesy of iStock. Image available here: http://www.istockphoto.com/vector/moses-destroying-the-ten-commandments-and-golden-calf-26526173?st=583c6b3

p. 69—"A dreidel on its side…" by Thomas Cotsonas

p. 72—"US president Franklin Roosevelt in wheelchair due to Polio poliomyelitis" released into the public domain by American Political History via Wikimedia Commons. The image was "renamed and uploaded by "User: Jollyroger." Image available here. https://commons.wikimedia.org/wiki/File:Rooseveltinwheelchair.jpg Public Domain, https://commons.wikimedia.org/w/index.php?curid=881143

p. 74—By Geoff Stearns – Flickr: Laguardia Sunset, CC BY 2.0, https://commons.wikimedia.org/w/index.php?curid=28284385

p. 77—"Jones Beach Water Tower" by kgdesigns, courtesy of iStock. Image available here: http://www.istockphoto.com/photo/jones-beach-water-tower-534985?st=caco125

p. 79—"Present-day Washington Square Park…" by Thomas Cotsonas

p. 81—"Spaghetti dish…" by Thomas Cotsonas

p. 83—"Luna Island, Niagara, Falls, N.Y.," by Detroit Publishing Company, between 1900 and 1910. The image is in the public domain, and part of the Library of Congress' Prints and Photographs Division. Digital ID: (digital file from original) det 4a24370 http://hdl.loc.gov/loc.pnp/det.4a24370

p. 85—"The Unisphere in Flushing Meadows (present-day)" by Thomas Cotsonas

p. 87—"Mosaic of Robert Moses" by Thomas Cotsonas

Personal
ACKNOWLEDGMENTS

The author wishes to thank the following people, each of whom helped make better the work herein: Joel Brouwer, Kellie Wells, Wendy Rawlings, Anne Panning, Steve Fellner, H. Scott Hestevold, John Crowley, and—especially—Michael Martone. Also: David Andrews, Lord Philipp Chandos, Jesse DeLong, Dara Ewing, Tessa Fontaine, Bill Fox, AB Gorham, Devin Gribbons, Christopher Hellwig, Joshua R. Helms, Robert Herzog, B. J. Hollars, Michael Mejia, Micaela Morrissette, Bradford Morrow, David Plick, Juan Carlos Reyes, Jessica Lee Richardson, Betsy Seymour, Lisa Tallin, Danilo Thomas, and Kevin Weidner. A special thanks goes out to Diane Goettel and Angela Leroux-Lindsey, and everyone at Black Lawrence Press.

Thanks as well to E.S. Bird Library, Drake Memorial Library, Amelia Gayle Gorgas Library, Butler Library, Egan's, the National Weather Service, and the Ontario, NY chapter of the PLG.

Lastly, the author thanks his three brothers and his parents.

Photo: Karina Palafox

Thomas Cotsonas was born and raised in Rochester, New York. His writing has appeared in *Web Conjunctions, Western Humanities Review, Construction,* and other journals. *Nominal Cases,* his first book of fiction, is the recipient of the 2014 St. Lawrence Book Award. He teaches creative writing in the Writers House at Rutgers University and lives in New York City.